AF539895

TEXTBOOK OF DENDROCHRONOLOGY

Dr. Shubhrata R. Mishra
Dept. of Botany
Vikram University
Ujjain (M.P.)
(India)

DISCOVERY PUBLISHING HOUSE PVT. LTD.
NEW DELHI-110 002

First Published - 2010

Reprinted - 2015

ISBN: 978-81-8356-551-6

Textbook of Dendrochronology

Published by:

DISCOVERY PUBLISHING HOUSE PVT. LTD.

4383/4B, Ansari Road, Darya Ganj

New Delhi-110 002 (India)

Phone: +91-11-23279245, 43596064-65

Fax: +91-11-23253475

E-mail: discoverypublishinghouse@gmail.com

sales@discoverypublishinggroup.com

web: www.discoverypublishinggroup.com

Printed at:

Infinity Imaging Systems

Delhi

Preface

Dendrochronology (from Greek , *dendron*, "tree"; *khronos*, "time"; and , *-logia*) or tree-ring dating is the method of scientific dating based on the analysis of tree-ring growth patterns. This technique was developed during the first half of the 20th century originally by the astronomer A.E. Douglass, the founder of the Laboratory of Tree-Ring Research at the University of Arizona. Douglass sought to better understand cycles of sunspot activity and reasoned (correctly) that changes in solar activity would affect climate patterns on earth which would subsequently be recorded by tree-ring growth patterns (*i.e.*, sunspots ? climate ? tree rings). The technique of dendrochronology can date the tree rings in many types of wood to the exact calendar year each ring was formed.

Growth rings, also referred to as *tree rings* or *annual rings*, can be seen in a horizontal cross section cut through the trunk of a tree. Growth rings are the result of new growth in the vascular cambium, a lateral meristem, and are synonymous with secondary growth. Visible rings result from the change in growth speed through the seasons of the year, thus one ring usually marks the passage of one year in the life of the tree. The rings are more visible in temperate zones, where the seasons differ more markedly.

A benefit of dendrochronology is that it makes available specimens of once-living material accurately dated to a specific year to be used as a calibration and check of radiocarbon dating, through the estimation of a date range formed through the interception of radiocarbon (BP, or '**B**'efore '**P**'resent, where present equals 1950-01-01) and calendar years. The bristlecone pine, being exceptionally long-lived and slow growing, has been used for this purpose, with still-living and dead specimens providing tree ring patterns going back thousands of years. In some regions dating sequences of more than 10,000 years are available. The dendrochronologist faces many obstacles, however, including some species of ant which inhabit trees and extend their galleries into the wood, thus destroying ring structure.

—Author

Contents

1

INTRODUCTION

Dendrochronology (from Greek , *dendron*, "tree"; *khronos*, "time"; and , *-logia*) or tree-ring dating is the method of scientific dating based on the analysis of tree-ring growth patterns. This technique was developed during the first half of the 20th century originally by the astronomer A.E. Douglass, the founder of the Laboratory of Tree-Ring Research at the University of Arizona. Douglass sought to better understand cycles of sunspot activity and reasoned (correctly) that changes in solar activity would affect climate patterns on earth which would subsequently be recorded by tree-ring growth patterns (*i.e.*, sunspots→climate →tree rings). The technique of dendrochronology can date the tree rings in many types of wood to the exact calendar year each ring was formed.

Growth Rings

Growth rings, also referred to as *tree rings* or *annual rings*, can be seen in a horizontal cross section cut through the trunk of a tree. Growth rings are the result of new growth in the vascular cambium, a lateral meristem, and are synonymous with secondary growth. Visible rings result from the change in growth speed through the seasons of the year, thus one ring usually marks the passage of one year in the life of the tree. The rings are more visible in temperate zones, where the seasons differ more markedly.

The inner portion of a growth ring is formed early in the growing season, when growth is comparatively rapid (hence the wood is less dense) and is known as "early wood" or "spring wood" or "late-spring wood". The outer portion is the "late wood" (and has sometimes been termed "summer wood", often being produced in the summer, though sometimes in the autumn) and is denser. "Early wood" is used in preference to "spring wood", as the latter term may not correspond to that time of year in climates where early wood is formed in the early summer (e.g. Canada) or in autumn, as in some Mediterranean species.

Many trees in temperate zones make one growth ring each year, with the newest adjacent to the bark. For the entire period of a tree's life, a year-by-year record or ring pattern is formed that reflects the climatic conditions in which the tree grew. Adequate moisture and a long growing season result in a wide ring. A drought year may result in a very narrow one. Alternating poor and favorable conditions, such as mid summer droughts, can result in several rings forming in a given year. Trees from the same region will tend to develop the same patterns of ring widths for a given period. These patterns can be compared and matched ring for ring with trees growing in the same geographical zone and under similar climatic conditions. Following these tree-ring patterns from living trees back through time, chronologies can be built up, both for entire regions, and for sub-regions of the world. Thus wood from ancient structures can be matched to known chronologies (a technique called *cross-dating*) and the age of the wood determined precisely. Cross-dating was originally done by visual inspection, until computers were harnessed to do the statistical matching.

To eliminate individual variations in tree ring growth, dendrochronologists take the smoothed average of the tree ring widths of multiple tree samples to build up a ring history. This process is termed replication. A tree ring history whose beginning and end dates are not known is called a *floating chronology*. It can be anchored by cross-matching either the beginning or the end section against the end sections of another chronology (tree ring history) whose dates are known. Fully anchored chronologies which extend back more than 10,000 years exist for river oak trees from South Germany (from the Main and Rhine rivers). Another fully anchored chronology which extends back 8500 years exists for the bristlecone pine in the Southwest US (White Mountains of California). Furthermore, the mutual consistency of these two independent dendrochronological sequences has been confirmed by comparing their radiocarbon and dendrochronological ages. In 2004 a new calibration curve *INTCAL04* was internationally ratified for calibrated dates back to 26,000 Before Present (BP) based on an agreed worldwide data set of trees and marine sediments.

Sampling and Dating

Timber core samples measure the width of annual growth rings. By taking samples from different sites and different strata within a particular region, researchers can build a comprehensive historical sequence that becomes a part of the scientific record; for example, ancient timbers found in buildings can be dated to give an indication of when the source tree was alive and growing, setting an upper limit on the age of the wood. Some genera of trees are more suitable than others for this type of analysis. Likewise, in areas where trees grew in marginal conditions such as aridity or semi-aridity, the techniques of dendrochronology are more consistent than in humid areas. These tools have been important in archaeological dating of timbers of the cliff dwellings of Native Americans in the arid Southwest.

A benefit of dendrochronology is that it makes available specimens of once-living material accurately dated to a specific year to be used as a calibration and check of radiocarbon dating, through the estimation of a date range formed through the interception of radiocarbon (BP, or '**B**'efore '**P**'resent, where present equals 1950-01-01) and calendar years. The bristlecone pine, being exceptionally long-lived and slow growing, has been used for this purpose, with still-living and dead specimens providing tree ring patterns going back thousands of years. In some regions dating sequences of more than 10,000 years are available. The dendrochronologist faces many obstacles, however, including some species of ant which inhabit trees and extend their galleries into the wood, thus destroying ring structure.

Similar seasonal patterns also occur in ice cores and in varves (layers of sediment deposition in a lake, river, or sea bed). The deposition pattern in the core will vary for a frozen-over lake versus an ice-free lake,and with the fineness of the sediment. These are used for dating in a manner similar to dendrochronology, and such techniques are used in combination with dendrochronology, to plug gaps and to extend the range of the seasonal data available to archaeologists.

While archaeologists can use the technique to date the piece of wood and when it was felled, it may be difficult to definitively determine the age of a building or structure that the wood is in. The wood could have been reused from an older structure, may have been felled and left for many years before use, or could have been used to replace a damaged piece of wood.

Application

European chronologies derived from wooden structures found it difficult to bridge the gap in the 14th century when there was a building hiatus which coincided with the Black Death. Other plagues which were less well recorded also appear in the record. In areas where the climate is reasonably predictable, trees develop annual rings of different properties depending on weather, rain, temperature, etc. in different years. These variations may be used to infer past climate variations.

Given a sample of wood, the variation of the tree ring growths provides not only a match by year, it can also match location because the climate across Europe is not consistent. This makes it possible to determine the source of ships as well as smaller artifacts made from wood but which were transported long distances.

Principles of Dendrochronology

As with any science, dendrochronology is governed by a set of principles or "scientific rules." These principles have their roots as far back as 1785 (the Principle of Uniformitarianism) and as recent as 1987 (the Principle of Aggregate Tree Growth). Some are specific to dendrochronology while others, like the Principle of Replication, are basic to many disciplines. All tree-ring research must adhere to these principles, or else the research could be flawed. However, before one can understand the principles, one needs to know basic definitions of terms used in tree-ring research.

Tree ring: A layer of wood cells produced by a tree or shrub in one year, usually consisting of thin-walled cells formed early in the growing season (called *earlywood*) and thicker-walled cells produced later in the growing season (called *latewood*). The beginning of earlywood formation and the end of the latewood formation form one annual ring, which usually extends around the entire circumference of the tree.

Tree-ring chronology: A series of measured tree-ring properties, such as tree-ring width or maximum latewood density, that has been converted to dimensionless indices through the process of *standardization*. A tree-ring chronology therefore represents departures of growth for any one year compared to average growth. For example, an index of 0.75 (or 75) for a given year indicates growth below normal (indicated by 1.00, or 100).

Standardization: The process that removes undesirable long-term variations from a time series of measured tree-ring properties by dividing the actual measurements by those predicted from a statistically derived equation that relates tree growth over time to tree age. Usually this process tries to remove the growth trends due to normal physiological aging processes and changes in the surrounding forest community.

Increment borer: An auger-like instrument with a hollow shaft that is screwed into the trunk of a tree, and from which an increment core (or tree core) is extracted using an extractor (a long spoon inserted into the shaft that pulls out the tree core). These instruments are quite expensive, normally ranging from $200 to $500.

The Uniformitarian Principle

This principle states that physical and biological processes that link current environmental processes with current patterns of tree growth must have been in operation in the past. In other words, "the present is the key to the past," originally stated by James Hutton in 1785. However, dendrochronology adds a new "twist" to this principle: "the past is the key to the future." In other words, by knowing environmental conditions that operated in the past (by analyzing such conditions in tree rings), we can better predict and/or manage such environmental conditions in the future. Hence, by knowing what the climate-tree growth relationship is in the 20th century, we can reconstruct climate from tree rings well before weather records were ever kept!

For example, the graph above shows a long-term precipitation reconstruction for northern New Mexico based on tree rings (click on the image to see an enlarged version of the graph). The reconstruction was developed by calibrating the widths of tree rings from the 1900s with rainfall records from the 1900s. Because we assume that conditions must have been similar in the past, we can then use the widths of tree rings as a *proxy* (or substitute) for actual rainfall amounts prior to the historical record.

The Principle of Limiting Factors

As used in dendrochronology, this principle states that rates of plant processes are constrained by the primary environmental variable that is most limiting. For example, precipitation is often the most limiting factor to plant growth in arid and semiarid areas. In these regions, tree growth cannot proceed faster than that allowed by the amount of precipitation, causing the width of the rings (*i.e.*, the volume of wood produced) to be a function of precipitation. In some locations, rainfall is not the most limiting factor. For example, in the higher latitudes, temperature is often the most limiting factor that affects tree growth rates. In addition, the factor that is most limiting is often acted upon by other non-climatic factors. While precipitation may be limiting in semiarid regions, the effects of the low precipitation amounts may be compounded by well-drained (e.g. sandy) soils.

The Principle of Aggregate Tree Growth

This principle states that any individual tree-growth series can be "decomposed" into an aggregate of environmental factors, both human and natural, that affected the patterns of tree growth over time. For example, tree-ring growth (R) in any one year (indicated by a small "*t*", where *t* could be "1" for year 1, and "2" for year 2, etc.) is a function of an aggregateoffactors:

1. the age related growth trend (A) due to normal physiological aging processes;
2. the climate (C) that occurred during that year;
3. the occurrence of disturbance factors *within* the forest stand (for example, a blow down of trees), indicated by D1;
4. the occurrence of disturbance factors from *outside* the forest stand (for example, an insect outbreak that defoliates the trees, causing growth reduction), indicated by D2; and
5. random (error) processes (E) not accounted for by these otherprocesses.

(The Greek letter in front of D1 and D2 indicates either a "0" for absence or "1" for presence of the disturbance signal.) Therefore, to maximize the desired environmental signal being studied, the other factors should be minimized. For example, to maximize the climate signal, the age related trend should be removed, and trees and sites selected to minimize the possibility of internal and external ecological processes affecting tree growth.

The Principle of Ecological Amplitude

This principle states that a tree species "may grow and reproduce over a certain range of habitats, referred to as its *ecological amplitude*". For example, ponderosa pine (*Pinus ponderosa*) is the most widely distributed of all pine species in North America, growing in a diverse range of habitats. Therefore, ponderosa pine has a wide ecological amplitude. Conversely, giant sequoia trees (*Sequoiadendron giganteum*) grow in restricted areas on the western slopes of the Sierra Nevada of California. Therefore, this species has a narrow ecological amplitude. This principle is important because individual trees that are most useful to dendrochronology are often found near the *margins* of their natural range, latitudinally, longitudinally, and elevationally. The diagram above shows the different forest types as one increases elevation along a mountainside. To maximize the climate information available in ponderosa pine tree rings, we would likely sample trees at their *lower* elevational limit around 7000 feet (2130 metres).

The Principle of Site Selection

This principle states that sites useful to dendrochronology can be identified and selected based on criteria that will produce tree-ring series sensitive to the environmental variable being examined. For example, trees that are especially responsive to drought conditions can usually be found where rainfall is limiting, such as rocky outcrops, or on ridgecrests of mountains. Therefore, a dendrochronologist interested in past drought conditions would purposely sample trees growing in locations known to be water-limited. Sampling trees growing in low-elevation, mesic (wet) sites would not produce tree-ring series especially sensitive to rainfall deficits. The dendrochronologist *must* select sites that will maximize the environmental signal being investigated. In the figure below, the tree on the left is growing in an environment that produced a *complacent* series of tree rings.

The Principle of Crossdating

This principle states that matching patterns in ring widths or other ring characteristics (such as ring density patterns) among several tree-ring series allow the identification of the exact year in which each tree ring was formed. For example, one can date the construction of a building, such as a barn or Indian pueblo, by matching the tree-ring patterns of wood taken from the buildings with tree-ring patterns from living trees. Crossdating is considered the fundamental principle of dendrochronology - without the precision given by crossdating, the dating of tree rings would be nothing more than simple ring counting!

The Principle of Replication

This principle states that the environmental signal being investigated can be maximized, and the amount of "noise" minimized, by sampling more than one stem radius per tree, and more than one tree per site. Obtaining more than one increment core per tree reduces the amount of "intra-tree variability", in other words, the amount of non-desirable environmental signal peculiar to only tree. Obtaining numerous trees from one site, and perhaps several sites in a region, ensures that the amount of "noise" (environmental factors not being studied, such as air pollution) is minimized.

The Uniformitarian Principle states that physical and biological processes that link current environmental processes with current patterns of tree growth must have been in operation in the past (after Fritts 1976). In other words, "the present is the key to the past," originally stated by James Hutton in 1785. However, dendrochronology adds a new "twist" to this principle: "the past is the key to the future." In other words, by knowing environmental conditions that operated in the past (by analyzing such conditions in tree rings), we can better predict and/or manage such environmental conditions in the future.

The Principle of Limiting Factors states that rates of plant processes can occur only as fast as allowed by the factor that is most limiting. For example, if rainfall is the most limiting factor, then the amount of wood produced by a tree in any single year will reflect mostly the amount of rainfall that fell within that year.

The Principle of Aggregate Tree Growth states that any individual tree-growth series can be "decomposed" into an aggregate of environmental factors, both human and natural, that affected the patterns of tree growth over time. For example, tree-ring growth in any one year is a function of an aggregate of factors:

- the age related growth trend due to normal physiological aging processes;
- the climate that occurred during that year the occurrence of factors *within* the forest stand (for example, a blow down of trees);
- the occurrence of factors from *outside* the forest stand (for example, an insect outbreak that defoliates the trees, causing growth reduction);
- random (error) processes not accounted for by these other processes.

Therefore, to maximize the desired environmental signal being studied, the other factors should be minimized. For example, to maximize the climate signal, the age related trend should be removed, and trees and sites selected to minimize the possibility of internal and external ecological processes affecting tree growth. Simple, right?

The Principle of Ecological Amplitude states that species may grow, reproduce, and propagate across wide, narrow, or restricted ranges of habitats. For example, ponderosa pine (Pinus ponderosa) is the most widely distributed of all pine species in North America, growing in a diverse range of habitats (wet, dry, low elevation, and high elevation). Therefore, ponderosa pine has a wide ecological amplitude. Conversely, giant sequoia trees (Sequoiadendron giganteum) grow in restricted areas on the western slopes of the Sierra Nevada of California. Giant sequoia, therefore, has a narrow ecological amplitude. This principle is important because tree species useful to dendrochronology are often found near the margins of their natural range, such as white spruce trees (Picea glauca) near the upper latitudinal treeline.

The Principle of Site Selection states that sites useful to dendrochronology can be identified and selected based on criteria that will produce tree-ring series sensitive to the environmental variable being examined. For example, trees that are especially responsive to drought conditions can usually be found where rainfall is limiting, such as rocky outcrops, or on ridgecrests of mountains. Therefore, a dendrochronologist interested in past drought conditions would purposely sample trees growing in locations known to be water-limited. Sampling trees growing in low-elevation, mesic (wet) sites would not produce tree-ring series especially sensitive to rainfall deficits. The dendrochronologist must select sites that will maximize the environmental signal being investigated.

The Principle of Crossdating states that matching patterns in ring widths or other ring characteristics (such as ring density patterns) among several tree-ring series allow the identification of the exact year in which each tree ring was formed. For example, one can date the construction of a building, such as a barn or

Indian pueblo, by matching the tree-ring patterns of wood taken from the buildings with tree-ring patterns from living trees.

The Principle of Replication states that the environmental signal being investigated can be maximized, and the amount of "noise" minimized, by sampling more than one stem radius per tree, and more than one tree per site. Obtaining more than one increment core per tree reduces the amount of "intra-tree variability", in other words, the amount of non-desirable environmental signal peculiar to only tree. Obtaining numerous trees from one site, and perhaps several sites in a region, ensures that the amount of "noise" (environmental factors not being studied, such as air pollution) is minimized.

2

What Are Trees?

INTRODUCTION

A tree is a perennial woody plant. It is most often defined as a woody plant that has many secondary branches supported clear of the ground on a single main stem or trunk with clear apical dominance. A minimum height specification at maturity is cited by some authors, varying from 3 m to 6 m; some authors set a minimum of 10 cm trunk diameter (30 cm girth) Woody plants that do not meet these definitions by having multiple stems and/or small size, are called shrubs. Compared with most other plants, trees are long-lived, some reaching several thousand years old and growing to up to 115 m (379 ft) high.

Trees are an important component of the natural landscape because of their prevention of erosion and the provision of a weather-sheltered ecosystem in and under their foliage. Trees also play an important role in producing oxygen and reducing carbon dioxide in the atmosphere, as well as moderating ground temperatures. They are also elements in landscaping and agriculture, both for their aesthetic appeal and their orchard crops (such as apples). Wood from trees is a building material, as well as a primary energy source in many developing countries. Trees also play a role in many of the world's mythologies.

Classification

A tree is a plant form that occurs in many different orders and families of plants. Trees show a variety of growth forms, leaf type and shape, bark characteristics, and reproductive organs.

The tree form has evolved separately in unrelated classes of plants, in response to similar environmental challenges, making it a classic example of parallel evolution. With an estimate of 100,000 tree species, the number of tree species worldwide might total 25 percent of all living plant species. The majority of tree species grow in tropical regions of the world and many of these areas have not been surveyed yet by botanists, making species diversity and ranges poorly understood.

The earliest trees were tree ferns and horsetails, which grew in forests in the Carboniferous Period; tree ferns still survive, but the only surviving horsetails are not of tree form. Later, in the Triassic Period, conifers, ginkgos, cycads and other gymnosperms appeared, and subsequently flowering plants in the Cretaceous Period. Most species of trees today are flowering plants (Angiosperms) and conifers. The listing below gives examples of well-known trees and how they are classified.

A small group of trees growing together is called a grove or copse, and a landscape covered by a dense growth of trees is called a forest. Several biotopes are defined largely by the trees that inhabit them; examples are rainforest and taiga . A landscape of trees scattered or spaced across grassland (usually grazed or burned over periodically) is called a savanna. A forest of great age is called old growth forest or ancient woodland (in the U.K.). A young tree is called a sapling.

Morphology

The parts of a tree are the roots, trunk(s), branches, twigs and leaves. Tree stems consist mainly of support and transport tissues (*xylem* and *phloem*). Wood consists of *xylem* cells, and bark is made of *phloem* and other tissues external to the vascular cambium. Trees may be grouped into *exogenous* and *endogenous* trees according to the way in which their stem diameter increases. Exogenous trees, which comprise the great majority of trees (all conifers, and almost all broadleaf trees), grow by the addition of new wood outwards, immediately under the bark. Endogenous trees, mainly in the monocotyledons (e.g., palms and dragon trees), but also cacti, grow by addition of new material inwards.

As an exogenous tree grows, it creates growth rings as new wood is laid down concentrically over the old wood. In species growing in areas with seasonal climate changes, wood growth produced at different times of the year may be visible as alternating light and dark, or soft and hard, rings of wood n temperate climates, and tropical climates with a single wet-dry season alternation, the growth rings are annual, each pair of light and dark rings being one year of growth; these are known as annual rings. In areas with two wet and dry seasons each year, there may be two pairs of light and dark rings each year; and in some (mainly semi-desert regions with irregular rainfall), there may be a new growth ring with each rainfall. In tropical rainforest regions with constant year-round climate, growth is continuous and the growth rings are not visible with no change in the wood texture. In species with annual rings, these rings can be counted to determine the age of the tree, and used to date cores or even wood taken from trees in the past, a practice is known as the science of dendrochronology. Very few tropical trees can be accurately aged in this manner. Age determination is also impossible in endogenous trees.

The roots of a tree are generally embedded in earth, providing anchorage for the above-ground biomass and absorbing water and nutrients from the soil. It should be noted, however, that while ground nutrients are essential to a tree's growth the majority of its biomass comes from carbon dioxide absorbed from the atmosphere (see photosynthesis). Above ground, the trunk gives height to the leaf-bearing branches, aiding in competition with other plant species for sunlight. In many trees, the arrangement of the branches optimizes exposure of the leaves to sunlight.

Not all trees have all the plant organs or parts mentioned above. For example, most palm trees are not branched, the saguaro cactus of North America has no functional leaves, tree ferns do not produce bark, etc. Based on their general shape and size, all of these are nonetheless generally regarded as trees. A plant form that is similar to a tree, but generally having smaller, multiple trunks and/or branches that arise near the ground, is called a shrub. However, no precise differentiation between shrubs and trees is possible. Given their small size, bonsai plants would not technically be 'trees', but one should not confuse reference to the form of a species with the size or shape of individual specimens. A spruce seedling does not fit the definition of a tree, but all spruces are trees.

Record Breaking Trees

The world's champion trees can be rated on height, trunk diameter or girth, total size, and age. It is significant that in each case, the top position is always held by a conifer, though a different species in each case; in most measures, the second to fourth places are also held by conifers.

Tallest Trees

The heights of the tallest trees in the world have been the subject of considerable dispute and much exaggeration. Modern verified measurement with laser rangefinders combined with tape drop measurements made by tree climbers, carried out by the U.S. Eastern Native Tree Society has shown that some older measuring methods and measurements are often unreliable, sometimes producing exaggerations of 5% to 15% above the real height. Historical claims of trees of 130 m (427 ft), and even 150 m (492 ft), are now largely disregarded as unreliable, and attributed to human error. (however, see "Tallest specimens" chapter in *Eucalyptus regnans* article). Historical records of fallen trees measured prostrate on the ground are considered to be far more reliable. The following are now accepted as the top five tallest reliably measured species in recent years:

- Coast Redwood (*Sequoia sempervirens*): 115.55 m (379.1 ft), Redwood National Park, California, United States
- Australian Mountain-ash (*Eucalyptus regnans*): 101.0 m (331.4 ft), south of Hobart, Tasmania, Australia

- Coast Douglas-fir (*Pseudotsuga menziesii*): 99.4 m (326.1 ft), Brummit Creek, Coos County, Oregon, United States
- Sitka Spruce (*Picea sitchensis*): 96.7 m (317.3 ft), Prairie Creek Redwoods State Park, California, United States
- Giant Sequoia (*Sequoiadendron giganteum*): 94.9 m (311.4 ft), Redwood Mountain Grove, Kings Canyon National Park, California, United States.

Stouest Tree

The girth of a tree is much easier to measure than the height, as it is a simple matter of stretching a tape round the trunk, and pulling it taut to find the circumference. Despite this, UK tree author Alan Mitchell made the following comment about measurements of yew trees:

> "The aberrations of past measurements of yews are beyond belief. For example, the tree at Tisbury has a well-defined, clean, if irregular bole at least 1.5 m long. It has been found to have a girth which has dilated and shrunk in the following way: 11.28 m (1834 Loudon), 9.3 m (1892 Lowe), 10.67 m (1903 Elwes and Henry), 9.0 m (1924 E. Swanton), 9.45 m (1959 Mitchell). ...Earlier measurements have therefore been omitted."

As a general standard, tree girth is taken at 'breast height'; this is defined differently in different situations, with most forestry measurements taking girth at 1.3 m above ground, while those who measure ornamental trees usually measure at 1.5 m above ground; in most cases this makes little difference to the measured girth. On sloping ground, the "above ground" reference point is usually taken as the highest point on the ground touching the trunk, but some use the average between the highest and lowest points of ground [*citation needed*]. Some of the inflated old measurements may have been taken at ground level. Some past exaggerated measurements also result from measuring the complete next-to-bark measurement, pushing the tape in and out over every crevice and buttress.

Modern trends are to cite the tree's diameter rather than the circumference; this is obtained by dividing the measured circumference by p; it assumes the trunk is circular in cross-section (an oval or irregular cross-section would result in a mean diameter slightly greater than the assumed circle). This is cited as dbh (diameter at breast height) in tree and forestry literature.

One further problem with measuring baobabs *Adansonia* is that these trees store large amounts of water in the very soft wood in their trunks. This leads to marked variation in their girth over the year, swelling to a maximum at the end of the rainy season, minimum at the end of the dry season. Although baobabs have some of the highest girth measurements of any trees, no accurate measurements are available, but probably do not exceed 10-11 m (33–36 ft) diameter.

The stoutest living single-trunk species in diameter, excluding baobabs, are:

- Montezuma Cypress *Taxodium mucronatum*: 11.62 m (38.1 ft), Árbol del Tule, Santa Maria del Tule, Oaxaca, Mexico Note though that this diameter includes buttressing; the actual idealised diameter of the area of its wood is 9.38 m (30.8 ft)
- Giant Sequoia *Sequoiadendron giganteum*: 8.85 m (29 ft), General Grant tree, Grant Grove, California, United States
- Coast Redwood *Sequoia sempervirens*: 7.44 m (24.4 ft), Prairie Creek Redwoods State Park, California, United States.

Charles Darwin reported finding *Fitzroya cupressoides* with trunk circumferences of up to 40 m (130 ft) implying a diameter of about 12 m (40 ft), but this may be an anomaly as the largest known measurements are about 5 m.

An addition problem lies in cases where multiple trunks (whether from an individual tree or multiple trees) grow together. The Sacred Fig is a notable example of this, forming additional 'trunks' by growing adventitious roots down from the branches, which then thicken up when the root reaches the ground to form new trunks; a single Sacred Fig tree can have hundreds of such trunks. Occasionally, errors may occur due to confusion between girth (circumference) and diameter.

Largest Trees

The largest trees in total volume are those which are both tall and of large diameter, and in particular, which hold a large diameter high up the trunk. Measurement is very complex, particularly if branch volume is to be included as well as the trunk volume, so measurements have only been made for a small number of trees, and generally only for the trunk. No attempt has ever been made to include root volume. Measuring standards vary.

The top four species measured so far are:

- Giant Sequoia *Sequoiadendron giganteum*: 1,487 m³ (52,508 cu ft), General Sherman
- Coast Redwood *Sequoia sempervirens*: 1,203 m³ (42,500 cu ft), Lost Monarch
- Western Redcedar *Thuja plicata*: 500 m³ (17,650 cu ft), Quinault Lake Redceda
- Kauri *Agathis australis*: circa 400 m³ (15,000 cu ft), Tane Mahuta tree otal volume, including branches, 516.7 m³/ 18,247 cu ft)

However, the Alerce *Fitzroya cupressoides*, as yet unmeasured, may well slot in at third or fourth place, and Montezuma Cypress *Taxodium mucronatum* and other giants are also likely to be high in the list. The largest angiosperm tree is currently a Tasmanian Blue Gum (*Eucalyptus globulus*) in Tasmania, with a volume of 368 m³.

Oldest Trees

The oldest trees are determined by growth rings, which can be seen if the tree is cut down or in cores taken from the edge to the center of the tree. Accurate determination is only possible for trees which produce growth rings, generally those which occur in seasonal climates; trees in uniform non-seasonal tropical climates grow continuously and do not have distinct growth rings. It is also only possible for trees which are solid to the center of the tree; many very old trees become hollow as the dead heartwood decays away. For some of these species, age estimates have been made on the basis of extrapolating current growth rates, but the results are usually little better than guesswork or wild speculation. White (1998) proposes a method of estimating the age of large and veteran trees in the United Kingdom through the correlation between a tree's stem diameter, growth character and age.

The verified oldest measured ages are:

- Norway Spruce *Picea abies*: 9,550 years arbon dating
- Great Basin Bristlecone Pine (Methuselah) *Pinus longaeva*: 4,844 years
- Alerce *Fitzroya cupressoides*: 3,622 years
- Giant Sequoia *Sequoiadendron giganteum*: 3,266 years
- Huon-pine *Lagarostrobos franklinii*: 2,500 years
- Rocky Mountains Bristlecone Pine *Pinus aristata*: 2,435 years.
- Other species suspected of reaching exceptional age include European Yew *Taxus baccata* (probably over 2,000 years and Western Redcedar *Thuja plicata*.
- The oldest reported age for an angiosperm tree is 2293 years for the Sri Maha Bodhi Sacred Fig (*Ficus religiosa*) planted in 288 BC at Anuradhapura, Sri Lanka; this is also the oldest human-planted tree with a known planting date.

The tree has always been a cultural symbol. Common icons are the World tree, for instance Yggdrasil, and the tree of life. The tree is often used to represent nature or the environment itself. A common misconception is that trees get most of their mass from the ground. Actually, 99% of a tree's mass comes from the air.

SEQUOIA

Sequoia sempervirens is the sole living species of the genus *Sequoia* in the cypress family Cupressaceae (formerly treated in Taxodiaceae). Common names include Coast Redwood and California Redwood (it is one of three species of trees known as redwoods, but "redwood" per se normally refers to this species). It is an evergreen, long-lived, monoecious tree living for up to 2200 years, and this species includes the tallest trees in the world, reaching up to 115.5 m (379.1 ft) in height and 8 m (26 ft) diameter at breast height.

The name "sequoia" is sometimes used as a general term for the subfamily Sequoioideae in which this genus is classified, together with *Sequoiadendron* (Giant Sequoia) and *Metasequoia* (Dawn Redwood); as a common name, it usually refers to *Sequoiadendron*.

Description

Coast redwoods have a conical crown, with horizontal to slightly drooping branches. The bark is very thick, up to 30 cm (12 in), and quite soft, fibrous with a bright red-brown when freshly exposed (hence the name 'redwood'), weathering darker. The root system is composed of shallow, wide-spreading lateral roots. The leaves are variable, being 15-25 mm long and flat on young trees and shaded shoots in the lower crown of old trees, and scale-like, 5-10 mm long on shoots in full sun in the upper crown of older trees; there is a full range of transition between the two extremes. They are dark green above, and with two blue-white stomatal bands below. Leaf arrangement is spiral, but the larger shade leaves are twisted at the base to lie in a flat plane for maximum light capture. The seed cones are ovoid, 15-32 mm long, with 15-25 spirally arranged scales; pollination is in late winter with maturation about 8-9 months after. Each cone scale bears 3-7 seeds, each seed 3-4 mm long and 0.5 mm broad, with two wings 1 mm wide. The seeds are released when the cone scales dry out and open at maturity. The pollen cones are oval, 4-6 mm long. The species is monoecious, with pollen and seed cones on the same plant. Its genetic makeup is unusual among conifers, being a hexaploid (6n) and likely autoallopolyploid . The mitochondrial genome is (unlike other conifers) paternally inherited.

Range and Ecology

Coast Redwoods occupy a narrow strip of land approximately 750 km (470 miles) in length and 8-75 km (5-47 miles) in width along the Pacific coast of North America; the elevation range is mostly from 30-750 m, occasionally down to sea level and up to 920 m (about 3,000 feet) (Farjon 2005). They usually grow in the mountains where there is more precipitation from the incoming moisture off the ocean. The tallest and oldest trees are found in deep valleys and gullies, where year-round streams can flow, and fog drip is regular. The trees above the fog layer, above about 700 m, are shorter and smaller due to the drier, windier, and colder conditions. In addition, tanoak, pine and Douglas-fir often crowd out redwoods at these elevations. Few redwoods grow close to the ocean, due to intense salt spray, sand and wind.

The northern boundary of its range is marked by two groves on the Chetco River on the western fringe of the Klamath Mountains, 25 km (15 miles) north of the California-Oregon border. The largest (and tallest) populations are in Redwood National and State Parks (Del Norte and Humboldt Counties) and Humboldt Redwoods State Park (Humboldt County, California).

This native area provides a unique environment with heavy seasonal rains (of up to 2,500 mm or 100 inch annually). Cool coastal air and fog keep this forest consistently damp year round. Several factors, including the heavy rainfall, create a soil with less nutrients than are necessary, causing the trees to depend heavily on the entire biotic community of the forest, and complete recycling of the trees when dead. This forest community includes Coast Douglas-fir, Western Hemlock, Tanoak, Pacific Madrone, and other trees along with a wide variety of ferns, Redwood sorrel, mosses and mushrooms. Redwood forests provide habitat for a variety of mammals, birds, reptiles, and amphibians. Old growth redwood stands provide habitat for the federally threatened Spotted Owl and the California-endangered Marbled Murrelet.

The thick, tannin-rich bark, combined with foliage that starts high above the ground provides good protection from both fire and insect damage, contributing to the Coast Redwood's longevity. The oldest known Coast Redwood is about 2,200 years old many others in the wild exceed 600 years. The numerous claims of older trees are incorrect Interestingly enough, Coast Redwoods because of their seemingly timeless lifespan were deemed the "everlasting redwood" at the turn of the century; in Latin, "sempervirens" means "ever green" or "everlasting," a coincidence unbeknown to those who named these giants.

The prehistoric fossil range of the genus is considerably greater, with a subcosmopolitan distribution including Europe and Asia until about 5 million years ago.

Reproduction

Coast Redwood reproduces both sexually and asexually. Seed production begins at 10-15 years of age, and large seed crops occur frequently, but viability of the seed is low, typically well below 15%. The low viability may be an adaptation to discourage seed predators, which do not want to waste time sorting chaff (empty seeds) from edible seeds. The winged seeds are small and light, weighing 3.3-5 mg (200-300 seeds/g; 5,600-8,500/ounce). The wings are not effective for wide dispersal, and seeds are dispersed by wind an average of only 60-120 m (200-400 feet) from the parent tree. Growth of seedlings is very fast, with young trees known to reach 20 m (65 feet) tall in 20 years. Coast Redwoods can also reproduce asexually by layering or sprouting from the root crown, stump, or even fallen branches; if a tree falls over, it will regenerate a row of new trees along the trunk. This is the reason for many trees naturally growing in a straight line. Sprouts originate from dormant or adventitious buds at or under the surface of the bark. The dormant sprouts are stimulated when the main adult stem gets damaged or starts to die. Many sprouts spontaneously erupt and develop around the circumference of the tree trunk. Within a short period after sprouting, each sprout will develop its own root system, with the dominant sprouts forming a ring of trees around the parent root crown or stump. This ring of trees is called a "fairy ring". Sprouts can achieve heights of 2.3 m (8 feet) in a single growing season.

Redwoods may also reproduce using burls. A burl is a woody lignotuber that commonly appears on a redwood tree below the soil line, though when above, usually within 3 m of the soil. Burls are capable of sprouting into new trees when detached from the parent tree, though exactly how this happens is yet to be studied. Shoot clones commonly sprout from burls and are often turned into decorative hedges when found in suburbia.

The species is very tolerant of flooding and flood deposits, the roots rapidly growing into thick silt deposits after floods.

Cultivation and Uses

Coast Redwood is one of the most valuable timber species in California, with 899,000 acres (364,000 ha) of redwood forest, all second growth, managed for timber production. Coast Redwood lumber is highly valued for its beauty, light weight, and resistance to decay. Its lack of resin makes it resistant to fire.

Because of its impressive resistance to decay, redwood was extensively used for railroad ties and trestles throughout California. Many of the old ties have been recycled for use in gardens as borders, steps, etc. Redwood burls are used in the production of table tops, veneers, and turned goods.

The Coast Redwood is locally naturalized in New Zealand, notably at Rotorua. Other areas of successful cultivation outside of the native range include Great Britain, Italy, Portugal, the Queen Charlotte Islands, middle elevations of Hawaii, a small area in central Mexico (Jilotepec) and the southeastern United States from eastern Texas to Maryland.

Statistics

Trees over 60 m (200 feet) are common, and many are over 90 m (300 feet).

- The current tallest tree is Hyperion, measuring at 115.55 m (379.1 feet). The tree was discovered in Redwood National Park during Summer 2006 by Chris Atkins and Michael Taylor and has been measured as the world's tallest living thing. The previous record holder was the Stratosphere Giant in the Humboldt Redwoods State Park, at 112.83 m, last measured in 2004 (was 112.34 m in Aug 2000 and 112.56 m in 2002). Until it fell in March 1991, the "Dyerville Giant" was the record holder. It too stood in Humboldt Redwoods State Park; it was 113.4 metres high and estimated to be 1,600 years old.
- There are 15 known living trees more than 110 m (361 feet) tall.
- There are 47 trees that are more than 105 m (344.5 feet) tall.
- A tree claimed to be 115.8 m (380 feet) was cut down in 1912.
- The tallest non-redwood tree is a 101 m (331 foot) tall *Eucalyptus regnans*, dubbed Centurion, discovered near Hobart in Tasmania, Australia.

In 2004, an article in *Nature* reported that the theoretical maximum potential height of Coast Redwoods (or any other tree) is limited to between 122 and 130 m (between 400 and 425 feet), due to gravity and the friction between water and the vessels through which it flows.

The largest Coast Redwood in volume is the "Lost Monarch", with an estimated volume of 42,500 cubic feet; it is 320 feet tall with a diameter of 26 feet at breast high (DBH). It is located in the Grove of Titans. Among current living trees there are only 7 known Giant Sequoias that are larger; these are shorter, but have thicker trunks overall, giving the largest Giant Sequoia, General Sherman, a volume of 1,487 cubic metres (52,510 cubic feet), making it the world's largest known tree. A redwood cut down in 1926 had a claimed volume of 1,794 m^3 (63,350 cubic feet), but this is not verified.

About fifty 'albino' redwoods (mutant individuals that cannot manufacture chlorophyll) are known to exist, reaching heights of up to 20 m. These trees survive as parasites, obtaining food by grafting their root systems with those of normal trees. While similar mutations occur sporadically in other conifers, no cases are known of such individuals surviving to maturity in any other conifer species.

EUCALYPTUS REGNANS

It is an evergreen tree, and it is the tallest of the eucalypts, growing to 70-120 m (230-400 feet), with a straight, grey trunk, smooth-barked except for the rough basal 5-15 metres. The leaves are falcate (sickle-shaped) to lanceolate, 9-14 cm long and 1.5-2.5 cm broad, with a long acuminate apex and smooth margin, green to grey-green with a reddish petiole. The flowers are produced in clusters of 9-15 together, each flower about 1 cm diameter with a ring of numerous white stamens. The fruit is a capsule 5-9 mm long and 4-7 mm broad.

Habitat

It occurs in cool, deep soiled, mostly mountainous areas to 1000 m altitude with high rainfall of over 1200 mm per year. They grow very quickly, at more than a metre a year, and can reach 65 metres in 50 years, with an average life-span of 400 years. The fallen logs continue supporting a rich variety of life for centuries more on the forest floor.

Unusually for a eucalypt, it tends not to recover by re-shooting after fire, and regenerates only from seed. The seeds are released from their woody capsules (gumnuts) by heat and for successful germination the seedlings require a high level of light, much more than reaches the forest floor when there is a mature tree canopy. Severe fires can kill all the trees in a forest, prompting a massive release of seed to take advantage of the nutrients in the ash bed. Seedling densities of up to 2.5 million per hectare have been recorded after a major fire. Competition and natural thinning eventually reduces the mature tree density to about 30 to 40 individuals per hectare. Because it takes roughly 20 years for seedlings to reach sexual maturity, repeated fires in the same area can cause local extinctions. If, however, no fires regenerate an area, the trees die off after about 400 years and are replaced by other species.

Tallest Specimens

Eucalyptus regnans is the tallest of all flowering plants, and possibly the tallest of all plants, although no living specimens can make that claim. The tallest measured living specimen, named Centurion, stands 101 metres tall in Tasmania. Before the discovery of the Centurion, the tallest known specimen was Icarus Dream, which was rediscovered in Tasmania in January, 2005 and is 97 metres high. It was first measured by surveyors at 98.8 metres in 1962 but the documentation had been lost. 16 living trees in Tasmania have been reliably measured in excess of 90 metres.

Historically, the tallest individual is claimed to be the Ferguson Tree, at 132.6 metres, found in the Watts River region of Victoria in 1871 or 1872. This record is often disputed as unreliable, despite first-hand documentary evidence of it being measured on the ground by tape from a senior forestry official. Widespread agreement exists, however, that an exceptionally tall individual was reliably measured at 112.8 metres by theodolite in 1880 by a surveyor, George Cornthwaite, at Thorpdale, Victoria (the tree is known both as the Cornthwaite or Thorpdale Tree). When it was felled in 1881, Cornthwaite remeasured it on the ground by tape at 114.3 metres. The stump was commemorated with an insignificant plaque that exists today. That tree was about 1 metre shorter than the world's current tallest living tree, a Coast Redwood, 115.55 metres.

The tallest specimens encountered by early European settlers are now dead as a result of bushfires, logging and advanced age. Few living specimens exceed 90 metres; old records of logged trees make varied claims of extreme heights, but these are difficult to verify today.

Most of those claims come from Victoria: an acknowledged authority on tall and large trees, Professor Al Carder, notes that in 1888 a cash reward of 100 pounds was offered there for the discovery of any tree measuring more than 122 metres [400 feet]. The fact that such a considerable reward was never claimed is taken as evidence that such large trees did not exist. Carder's historical research, however, revealed that the reward was offered under conditions that made it highly unlikely to be collected. First, it was made in the depths of winter and applied only for a very short time. Next, the tree had to be measured by an accredited surveyor. Since loggers had already taken the largest trees from the most accessible Victorian forests, finding very tall trees then would have demanded an arduous trek into remote wilderness and at considerable altitude. In turn, that meant that searchers also needed the services of experienced bushmen to be able to guide them and conduct an effective search. Only one expedition actually penetrated one of the strongholds of *E. regnans* at Mount Baw Baw but its search was rendered ineffectual by cold and snow and managed to measure only a single living tree (the New Turkey Tree; 99.4 metres) before appalling conditions forced a retreat, Carder notes.

In 1911, a previously unknown report was discovered: it was written by a licensed surveyor, G.W. Robinson, who had kept his personal forestry records from six decades earlier during the 1850s in the Dandenong Ranges, near Melbourne. Robinson had arranged with loggers to notify him when they found a very tall tree, and noted that every one he measured exceeded 91 metres, the tallest being 104 metres. Robinson noted that the tallest trees were felled first and had no doubt that "some of the trees felled earlier would have measured quite some 400 feet [122 metres]".

Victoria's early State botanist, Ferdinand von Mueller, claimed to have personally measured one tree near the headwaters of the Yarra River at 122 metres. A government surveyor. David Boyle, claimed in 1862 to have measured a fallen tree in a deep gully in the Dandenongs at 119.5 metres, and with a diameter at its broken tip that indicated it might have lost another eight metres of trunk when it broke [128 metres in total]

The tops of the tallest trees are often snapped by wind: allowing for that in estimating an original height, however, presupposes that the break occurred in a hitherto undamaged tree. An alternate, and possibly more realistic scenario, is of a tree with several episodes of breakage and regrowth building up a stout stem without ever attaining the potential maximum height.

Von Mueller's early records also mention two trees on the nearby Black Spur Range, one alive and measuring 128 metres and another fallen tree said to measure 146 metres, but these were either based on hearsay or uncertain reliability. David Boyle also reported that a tree at Cape Otway measured 158 metres, but this too was based on hearsay.

Many prominent botanists and tree enthusiasts have long been sceptical of such claims because they lacked first-hand evidence from a credible source. But Carder notes that nor can all the claims can be considered imaginary: "The frequency, the persistence, and the wide occurrence of the reports leads to the belief that there was some basis of fact for the statements made."

None, however, had been verified by direct documentation until 1982 when Ken Simpendorfer, a Special Projects Officer for the Forests Commission, Victoria, directed a search of official Victorian archives. It unearthed a forgotten report from more than a century earlier, one that had not been referred to in other accounts of the species up to that time. It was written on 21 February 1872, by the Inspector of State Forests, William Ferguson, and was addressed to the Assistant Commissioner of Lands and

Surveys, Clement Hodgkinson. Ferguson had been instructed to explore and inspect the watershed of the Watts River and reported trees in great number and exceptional size in areas where loggers had not yet reached. He wrote:

> "In one instance I measured with a tape line one huge specimen that lay prostrate across a tributary of the Watts, and found it to be 435 feet [132.6 metres] from its root to the top of its trunk. At 5 feet from the ground it measures 18 feet in diameter, and at the extreme end where it has broken in its fall, it is 3 feet in diameter. This tree has been much burnt by fire, and I fully believe that before it fell it must have been more than 500 feet [152.4 metres] high. As it now lies, it forms a complete bridge across a deep ravine."

Carder concludes that the height limit for *E. regnans* is "not greatly over 300 feet now, but there is sound evidence that trees very much taller did indeed at one time stand".

It is also possible that individual trees will again attain such heights. Author Bob Beale has recorded that the tallest trees in the Black Spur Range now measure about 85 metres but - due to major bushfires in the 1920s and 30s - are less than 80 years old and have been growing consistently at the rate of about one metre a year.

Uses

Eucalyptus regnans is valued for its timber, and has been harvested in very large quantities. Primary uses are sawlogging and woodchipping. It was a major source of newsprint in the 20th century. Much of the present woodchip harvest is exported to Japan. While the area of natural stands with large old trees is rapidly decreasing, substantial areas of regrowth exist and it is increasingly grown in plantations, the long, straight, fast growing trunks being much more commercially valuable than the old growth timber.

It is a medium weight timber (about 680 kg/m^3) and rather coarse (stringy) in texture. Gum veins are common. The wood is easy to work and the grain is straight with long, clear sections without knots. The wood works reasonably well for steam-bending. Primary uses for sawn wood are furniture, flooring (where its very pale blonde colour is highly prized), panelling, veneer, plywood, window frames, general construction. The wood has sometimes been used for wood wool and cooperage. However, the wood needs steam reconditioning for high value applications, due to a tendency to collapse on drying. This wood is highly regarded by builders, furniture makers and architects.

Conservation

Great controversy surrounds the logging of old-growth *Eucalyptus regnans* in its natural range in both Victoria and Tasmania. Aside from its symbolic significance as the largest eucalypt of all, *Eucalyptus regnans* has value to conservationists in provides essential habitat to important birds and mammals (notably the Wedge tailed eagle, the Lyrebird and the endangered Victorian state animal emblem Leadbeater's Possum). In a land of vast, arid plains and desert, the contrasting lush fertility of mountain-ash forest is particularly dear to nature lovers.

Although its status as a species is secure, old-growth forests of *Eucalyptus regnans* are particularly susceptible to destruction by forestry. For this reason stands of very old and very tall trees exist only in pockets. Very few such stands of trees fall within those areas that have been listed as National Park or World Heritage environments. Most lie within areas controlled by state forestry management authorities and their heritage value is balanced against the commercial value of harvesting and then planting fast-growing and more productive monoculture timber crops on these comparatively well-watered and fertile areas.

In Tasmania, over 85% of old growth *regnans* forests have been logged. The trees continue to be clearfell logged by Gunns, a major forestry enterprise.

Political opposition to the logging of old-growth forests by the process known as clearfelling has grown very strong in recent years (particularly in the case of woodchipping), and the extent of future harvesting remains uncertain.

It has long been believed that while many species of eucalyptus successfully survived severe bushfires, forests of

Eucalyptus regnans are highly susceptible to destruction by fire. While the process of recovery of most eucalyptus forests is rapid, so that trees that are devoid of leaves may be fully foliaged within two years, in the case of *Eucalyptus regnans*, the recovery of a forest after a severe fire might require the total regrowth from seed of the devastated area, taking perhaps 200 years or more.

It has been suggested that fire is necessary for the germination of *Eucalyptus regnans*, and that young *Eucalyptus regnans* trees flourish best where there is open space, allowing sunlight to penetrate. Prior to European intervention, indigenous land management practices involved controlled burning in order to maintain grassland. This resulted in cleared areas in forests, around the peripheries of which young trees could germinate and grow. It is probable that these indigenous practices were used within forests of *Eucalyptus regnans*. Cleared spaces also occur naturally in tall forests when an old tree falls, or dies and loses its foliage. These very tall trees do not survive independently of each other, as single trees are more subject to lightening strikes and wind damage.

The natural habitat of the *Eucalyptus regnans* is in general the areas of Australia with the highest and most reliable precipitation. These areas are less prone to catastrophic fires than other forested areas. Research has indicated that a stand of Mountain Ash in Victoria is actually a multi-age stand due to fire, having experienced seven fires since the 1400s, whereas, since European settlement, many of Australia's Eucalyptus forests have suffered severe fires as often as every 20 years.

Studies conducted in the 20th by T.M. Cunningham and David H. Ashton suggest that the re-growth habit of *Eucalyptus regnans* requires open space, and an ash layer. For this reason clearfelling (as opposed to selective logging methods) can be justified for the successful germination and growth of seedlings, and, by hypothesis, the survival of the forest . The clearfell process can lead to spectacular and uniform regrowth of commercially viable timber, if managed properly. Those who support clearfelling see it as an ideal method of land management. Such arguments however completely overlook the impact of such activities on stream health, water yield of catchments, impacts on threatened forest fauna, and long term soil healthy and viability.

In addition to this, opponents of clearfelling point out that the forests survived for centuries without clearfelling and that it takes perhaps 300 years to replace a giant tree, commercially valuable only as woodchip, and therefore designated as "waste" by the harvesters. Opponents of clearfelling point out that the clearfell process was unavailable until the arrival of European settlers (indigenous people practised a mosaic burn system that kept the forest open but didn't remove large amounts of timber).

Half of Victoria's forested water catchment areas, which provides water requiring little treatment, are composed of *E. regnans* forest. Yields from these catchments fall significantly 20-40 years after disturbance, these areas have an increased risk of bushfire due to climate change

COAST DOUGLAS-FIR

The Coast Douglas-fir (*Pseudotsuga menziesii* var. *menziesii*), a variety of Douglas-fir, is an evergreen conifer native to the coastal regions of western North America, from west-central British Columbia, Canada southward to central California, United States. In Oregon and Washington its range is continuous from the Cascades crest west to the Pacific Ocean. In California, it is found in the Klamath and Coast Ranges as far south as the Santa Cruz Mountains, and in the Sierra Nevada as far south as the Yosemite region. It occurs from near sea level along the coast to 1,800 m (6,000 ft) in the Sierra Nevada. Further inland, Coast Douglas-fir is replaced by the related Rocky Mountain Douglas-fir (*Pseudotsuga menziesii* var. *glauca*).

Characteristics

Coast Douglas-fir is a very tall tree, the second-tallest conifer in the world (after Coast Redwood). Trees 60-75 m (200-250 feet) or more in height and 1.5-2 m (5-6 feet) in diameter are common in old growth stands, and maximum heights of 100-120 m (300-400 feet) with diameters up to 4.5-6m (14-18 feet) have been documented. The tallest living specimen is the "Doerner

Fir" (previously known as the Brummit fir), 100.3 m tall, at East Fork Brummit Creek in Coos County, Oregon, the stoutest is the "Queets Fir", 4.85 m diameter, in the Queets River valley, Olympic National Park, Washington. It commonly lives more than 500 years and occasionally more than 1,000 years.

The bark on young trees is thin, smooth, gray, and contains numerous resin blisters. On mature trees, it is 10-30 cm thick (4-12 inches) and corky. The shoots are brown to olive-green, turning gray-brown with age, smooth, though not as smooth as fir shoots, and finely pubescent with short dark hairs. The buds are a very distinctive narrow conic shape, 4-8 mm long, with red-brown bud scales. The leaves are spirally arranged but slightly twisted at the base to lie in flattish either side of the shoot, needle-like, 2-3.5 cm long, green above with no stomata, and with two whitish stomatal bands below. Unlike the Rocky Mountain Douglas-fir, Coast Douglas-fir foliage has a noticeable sweet fruity-resinous scent, particularly if crushed.

The mature female seed cones are pendent, 5-11 cm (2-4 inches) long, 2-3 cm broad when closed, opening to 4 cm broad. They are produced in spring, green at first, maturing orange-brown in the autumn 6-7 months later. The seeds are 5-6 mm long and 3-4 mm broad, with a 12-15 mm wing. The male (pollen) cones are 2-3 cm long, dispersing yellow pollen in spring.

In forest conditions, old individuals typically have a narrow, cylindric crown beginning 20-40 m (65-130 feet) above a branch-free trunk. Self-pruning is generally slow and trees retain their lower limbs for a long period. Young, open-grown trees typically have branches down to near ground level. It often takes 70-80 years for the trunk to be clear to a height of 5 m (17 ft) and 100 years to be clear to a height of 10 m (33 ft).

Appreciable seed production begins at 20-30 years in open-grown Coast Douglas-fir. Seed production is irregular; over a 5-7 year period, stands usually produce one heavy crop, a few light or medium crops, and one crop failure. Even during heavy seed crop years, only about 25 percent of trees in closed stands produce an appreciable number of cones. Each cone contains around 25 to 50 seeds. Seed size varies; average number of cleaned seeds varies from 70-88/g (32,000-40,000 per pound). Seeds from the northern portion of Coast Douglas-fir's range tend to be larger than seed from the south.

Ecology

Coast Douglas-fir is the dominant tree in the Pacific Northwest, occurring in nearly all forest types, competes well on most parent materials, aspects, and slopes. Adapted to a moist, mild climate, it grows larger and faster than Rocky Mountain Douglas-fir. Associated trees include Sitka Spruce, Sugar Pine, Western White Pine, Ponderosa Pine, Grand Fir, Coast Redwood, Western Redcedar, California Incense-cedar, Lawson's Cypress, Tanoak, Bigleaf Maple and several others. Pure stands are also common, particularly north of the Umpqua River in Oregon. Shrub associates in the central and northern part of Coast Douglas-fir's range include Vine Maple (*Acer circinatum*), Salal (*Gaultheria shallon*), Pacific Rhododendron (*Rhododendron macrophyllum*), Oregon-grape (*Mahonia aquifolium*), Red huckleberry (*Vaccinium parvifolium*), and Salmonberry (*Rubus spectabilis*). In the drier, southern portion of its range shrub associates include California Hazel (*Corylus cornuta* var. *californica*), Oceanspray (*Holodiscus discolor*), Creeping Snowberry (*Symphoricarpos mollis*), Western Poison-oak (*Toxicodendron diversilobum*), Ceanothus (*Ceanothus* spp.), and Manzanita (*Arctospaphylos* spp.). In wet coastal forests, nearly every surface of old-growth Coast Douglas-fir is covered by epiphytic mosses and lichens. It is sometimes parasitized by the Douglas-fir Dwarf Mistletoe. The rooting habit of Coast Douglas-fir is not particularly deep, with the roots tending to be shallower than those of same-aged Ponderosa Pine, Sugar Pine, or California Incense-cedar, though deeper than Sitka Spruce. Some roots are commonly found in organic soil layers or near the mineral soil surface.

Coast Douglas-fir seedlings are not a preferred browse of Black-tailed Deer and elk, but can be an important food source for these animals during the winter when other preferred forages are lacking. Douglas-fir seeds are an extremely important food for small mammals. Mice, voles, shrews, and chipmunks consumed an estimated 65 percent of a Douglas-fir seed crop following dispersal in western Oregon. The seeds are also important in the diets of the Pine Siskin, Song Sparrow, Golden-crowned Sparrow, White-crowned Sparrow, Red Crossbill, Dark-eyed Junco, and Purple Finch.

The Douglas squirrel harvests and caches great quantities of Douglas-fir cones for later use. They also eat mature pollen cones, developing inner bark, terminal shoots, and tender young needles.

Mature or "old-growth" Coast Douglas-fir is the primary habitat of the Red tree vole and the Spotted Owl. Home range requirements for breeding pairs of spotted owls are at least 400 ha (4 km²/1,000 acres) of old-growth. Red tree voles may also be found in immature forests if Douglas-fir is a significant component. This animal nests almost exclusively in the foliage of Douglas-fir trees. Nests are located 2-50 m (6-160 feet) above the ground. The red vole's diet consists chiefly of Coast Douglas-fir needles.

In many areas Coast Douglas-fir needles are a staple in the spring diet of Blue Grouse. In the winter, porcupines primarily eat the inner bark of young conifers, especially Douglas-fir. Douglas-fir snags are abundant in forests older than 100-150 years and provide cavity-nesting habitat for numerous forest birds.

The leaves are also used by the adelgid *Adelges cooleyi*; this 0.5 mm long sap-sucking insect is conspicuous on the undersides of the leaves by the small white "fluff spots" of protective wax that it produces. It is often present in large numbers, and can cause the foliage to turn yellowish from the damage in causes. Exceptionally, trees may be partially defoliated by it, but the damage is rarely this severe.

Forest Succession

The shade-intolerance of Douglas-fir plays a large role in the forest succession of lowland old growth communities of the Pacific Northwest. While mature stands of lowland old-growth forests contain many Western Hemlock (*Tsuga heterophylla*) seedlings, and some Western Redcedar (*Thuja plicata*) seedlings,

Douglas-fir dominated stands contain almost no Douglas-fir seedlings. This seeming contradiction occurs because Douglas-firs are intolerant of shade and rarely survive for long within the shaded understory.

When a tree dies in a mature forest the canopy opens up and sunlight becomes available as a source of energy for new growth. The shade-tolerant Western Hemlock seedlings that sprout beneath the canopy have a head-start on other seedlings. This competitive advantage allows the Western Hemlock to grow rapidly into the sunlight, while other seedlings still struggle to emerge from the soil. The boughs of the growing Western Hemlock limit the sunlight for smaller trees and severely limit the chances of shade-intolerant trees, such as the Douglas-fir. Over the course of centuries, Western Hemlock typically come to dominate the canopy of an old-growth lowland forest.

Douglas-firs are pioneer trees, and possess thicker bark and a somewhat faster growth rate than other climax trees of the area, such as the Western Hemlock and Western Redcedar. This quality often gives Douglas-firs a competitive advantage when the forest experiences a major disturbance such as fire. Periodically, portions of a Pacific Northwest lowland forest may be burned by wildfire, may be logged, or may be blown down by a wind-storm. These types of disturbances often create conditions where Douglas-firs have an advantage over less drought and fire-tolerant species.

Conifers dominate the climax forests of the Coastal Douglas-fir. All of the climax conifers that grow alongside Douglas-fir can live for centuries, with a few species capable of living for over a millennium. Forests that exist on this time scale experiences the type of sporadic disturbances that allow mature stands of Douglas-firs to establish themselves as a persistent element within a mature old-growth forest. When old growth forests survive in a natural state, they often look like a patchwork quilt of different forest communities. Western Hemlock typically dominate old growth forests, but contain sections of Douglas-firs, Redcedar, Alder, and even Redwood forests on their southern extent, near the Oregon and California border.

The logging practices of the last 200 years created artificial disturbances that caused Douglas-firs to thrive. The Douglas-fir's useful wood and its quick growth make it the crop of choice for many timber companies, which typically replant a clear-cut area with Douglas-fir saplings. The low-moisture conditions that exist within a clear-cut also naturally favor the regeneration of Douglas-fir. Because of clear-cut logging, almost all the Pacific Northwest forests not strictly set aside for protection are today dominated by Douglas-fir, while the normally dominant climax species, such as Western Hemlock and Western Redcedar are relatively rare.

Uses

Coast Douglas-fir is one of the worlds best timber producers and yields more timber than any other tree in North America. The wood is used for dimensional lumber, timbers, pilings, and plywood. Creosote treated pilings and decking are used in marine structures. The wood is also made into railroad ties, mine timbers, house logs, posts and poles, flooring, veneer, pulp, and furniture. Coast Douglas-fir is used extensively in landscaping. It is planted as a specimen tree or in mass screenings. It is also a popular Christmas tree.

PICEA SITCHENSIS

The Sitka Spruce (*Picea sitchensis*) is a large coniferous evergreen tree growing to 50-70 m tall, exceptionally to 100 m tall, and with a trunk diameter of up to 5 m, exceptionally to 6-7 m diameter. It is by far the largest species of spruce, and the third tallest conifer species in the world (after Coast Redwood and Coast Douglas-fir). It acquires its name from the community of Sitka, Alaska.

Bark is thin and scaly, flaking off in small circular plates 5-20 cm across. The crown is broad conic in young trees, becoming cylindric in older trees; old trees may have no branches in the lowest 30-40 m. The shoots are very pale buff-brown, almost white, and glabrous (hairless) but with prominent pulvini. The leaves are stiff, sharp and needle-like, 15-25 mm long, flattened in cross-section, dark glaucous blue-green above with two or three thin lines of stomata, and blue-white below with two dense bands of stomata.

The cones are pendulous, slender cylindrical, 5-11 cm long and 2 cm broad when closed, opening to 3 cm broad. They have thin, flexible scales 15-20 mm long; the bracts just above the scales are the longest of any spruce, occasionally just exserted and visible on the closed cones. They are green or reddish, maturing pale brown 5-7 months after pollination. The seeds are black, 3 mm long, with a slender, 7-9 mm long pale brown wing.

Sitka Spruce is native to the west coast of North America, with its northwestern limit on Kodiak Island, Alaska, and its southeastern limit near Fort Bragg in northern California. It is closely associated with the temperate rain forests and is found within a few kilometers of the coast in the southern portion of its range. North of Oregon, its range extends inland along river floodplains, but nowhere does its range extend more than 80 km from the Pacific Ocean and its inlets.

More than a century of logging has left only a remnant of the spruce forest. The largest trees were cut long before careful measurements could be made. Trees over 90 m tall may still be seen in the Pacific Rim National Park and Carmanah Walbran Provincial Park on Vancouver Island, British Columbia (the *Carmanah Giant*, at 96 meters (315 ft) tall the tallest tree in Canada), and in the Olympic National Park, Washington and Prairie Creek Redwoods State Park, California (USA); two at the last site are just over 96 meters (315 ft) tall. The *Queets Spruce* is the largest in the world with a trunk volume of 337 m³ (11,901 cubic feet). It is located near the Queets River in Olympic National Park, about 16 miles (26 km) from the Pacific Ocean. The fourth-largest tree, known as the *Seaside Spruce* or the *Klootchy Creek Giant*, with a height of 58.2 meters (191 ft) and a volume of 296 m³ (10,453 cubic feet lew down on December 2, 2007 during a windstorm, reducing it to 75 feet (23 m) tall. This was not unexpected as the tree had been hit by lightning and damaged in previous storms The *Quinault Lake Spruce* (pictured left) is the third largest in the world with a wood volume of 298 m³ (10,524 cubic feet). It is located near the eastern tip of Lake Quinault north of Aberdeen, Washington, about 24 miles (39 km) from the Pacific Ocean.

Sitka Spruce is a long-lived tree, with individuals over 700 years old known. Because it grows rapidly under favorable conditions, large size may not indicate exceptional age. The *Queets Spruce* has been estimated to be only 350 to 450 years old, but adds more than a cubic meter of wood each year.

A unique specimen with golden foliage that used to grow on the Queen Charlotte Islands, known as Kiidk'yaas, is sacred to the Haida Native American people. It was illegally felled, although saplings grown from cuttings can now be found near its original site.

Uses

Sitka Spruce is of major importance in forestry for timber and paper production. It is used widely in piano, harp, violin, and guitar manufacture, as its high strength-to-weight ratio and regular, knot-free rings make it an excellent conductor of sound. The Steinway & Sons piano company is well known for using exclusively Sitka Spruce soundboards in its pianos. The harp company, Lyon & Healy, is well known for its use of Sitka Spruce for the soundboard of their harps as well. For these reasons, the wood is an important material for sailing boat spars, homebuilt aircraft, and the nosecones of Trident missiles.

Outside of its native range, it is particularly valued for its fast growth on poor soils and exposed sites where few other trees can be grown successfully; in ideal conditions young trees may grow 1.5 m per year. It is naturalized in some parts of Ireland and Great Britain where it was introduced in 1831 (Mitchell, 1978) and New Zealand, though not so extensively as to be considered invasive. Sitka Spruce is also planted extensively in Denmark, Norway and Iceland. In Norway sitka spruce was introduced in the early 1900s. It has mainly been planted along the coast from Vest-Agder in the south to Troms in the north. It is more tolerant to wind and saline ocean air, and grows faster than the native Norwegian Spruce. It is estimated that 500 000 decare in Norway are planted with sitka spruce.

SEQUOIADENDRON

Sequoiadendron giganteum (Giant Sequoia, Sierra Redwood, or Wellingtonia) is the sole species in the genus *Sequoiadendron*, and one of three species of coniferous trees known as redwoods, classified in the family Cupressaceae in the subfamily Sequoioideae, together with *Sequoia sempervirens* (Coast Redwood) and *Metasequoia glyptostroboides* (Dawn Redwood). The common names "sequoia" and "redwood" generally refer to *Sequoiadendron* and the coast redwood, respectively.

Description

Giant Sequoias are the world's largest trees in terms of total volume (technically, only 6 living Giant Sequoia exceed the 42,500 cubic feet (1,200 m3) of the Lost Monarch Coast Redwood tree; see Largest trees). They grow to an average height of 50-85 m (165-280 ft) and 6-8 m (18-24 ft) in diameter. Record trees have been measured to be 94.8 m (311 ft) in height and 17 m (57 ft) in diameter. The oldest known Giant Sequoia based on ring count is 3,500 years old. Sequoia bark is fibrous, furrowed, and may be 90 cm (3 ft) thick at the base of the columnar trunk. It provides significant fire protection for the trees. The leaves are evergreen, awl-shaped, 3-6 mm long, and arranged spirally on the shoots. The seed cones are 4-7 cm long and mature in 18-20 months, though they typically remain green and closed for up to 20 years; each cone has 30-50 spirally arranged scales, with several seeds on each scale giving an average of 230 seeds per cone. The seed is dark brown, 4-5 mm long and 1 mm broad, with a 1 mm wide yellow-brown wing along each side. Some seed is shed when the cone scales shrink during hot weather in late summer, but most seeds are liberated when the cone dries out from fire heat and/or insect damage.

Giant Sequoia regenerates by seed. Trees up to about 20 years old may produce stump sprouts subsequent to injury. Giant Sequoia of all ages may sprout from the bole when old branches are lost to fire or breakage, but (unlike Coast Redwood) mature trees do not sprout from cut stumps. Young trees start to bear cones at the age of 12 years.

At any given time, a large tree may be expected to have approximately 11,000 cones. The upper part of the crown of any mature Giant Sequoia invariably produces a greater abundance of cones than its lower portions. A mature Giant Sequoia has been estimated to disperse from 300,000-400,000 seeds per year. The winged seeds may be carried up to 180m (600 ft) from the parent tree.

Lower branches die fairly readily from shading, but trees less than 100 years old retain most of their dead branches. Trunks of mature trees in groves are generally free of branches to a height of 20-50 m, but solitary trees will retain low branches.

Distribution

The natural distribution of Giant Sequoia is restricted to a limited area of the western Sierra Nevada, California. It occurs in scattered groves, with a total of 68 groves (see list of sequoia groves for a full inventory), comprising a total area of only 14,416 ha (144.16 km^2 or 35,607 acres). Nowhere does it grow in pure stands, although in a few small areas stands do approach a pure condition. The northern two-thirds of its range, from the American River in Placer County southward to the Kings River, has only eight disjunct groves. The remaining southern groves are concentrated between the Kings River and the Deer Creek Grove in southern Tulare County. Groves range in size from 1,240 ha (3,100 acres) with 20,000 mature trees, to small groves with only six living trees. Many are protected in Sequoia and Kings Canyon National Parks and Giant Sequoia National Monument.

Giant Sequoia is usually found in a humid climate characterized by dry summers and snowy winters. Most Giant Sequoia groves are on granitic-based residual and alluvial soils. The elevation of the Giant Sequoia groves generally ranges from 1,400-2,000 m (4,600-6,600 ft) in the north, and 1,700-2,150 m (5,600-7,000 ft) to the south. Giant Sequoia generally occurs on the south facing side of northern mountains, and on the northern face of more southern slopes.

High levels of reproduction are not necessary to maintain the present population levels. Few groves, however, have sufficient young trees to maintain the present density of mature Giant Sequoias for the future. The majority of Giant Sequoias are currently undergoing a gradual decline in density since the European settlement days.

Ecology

The Giant Sequoias are having difficulty reproducing in their original habitat (and very rarely reproduce in cultivation) due to the seeds only being able to grow successfully in mineral soils in full sunlight, free from competing vegetation. Although the seeds can germinate in moist needle humus in the spring, these seedlings will die as the duff dries in the summer. They therefore require periodic wildfire to clear competing vegetation and soil humus before successful regeneration can occur. Without fire, shade-loving species will crowd out young sequoia seedlings, and sequoia seeds will not germinate. When full grown, these trees typically require large amounts of water and are therefore often concentrated near streams.

Fires also bring hot air high into the canopy via convection, which in turn dries and opens the cones. The subsequent release of large quantities of seeds coincides with the optimal post-fire seedbed conditions. Loose ground ash may also act as a cover to protect the fallen seeds from ultraviolet radiation damage.

Due to fire suppression efforts and livestock grazing during the early and mid 20th century, low-intensity fires no longer occurred naturally in many groves, and still do not occur in some groves today. The suppression of fires also led to ground fuel build-up and the dense growth of fire-sensitive White Fir. This increased the risk of more intense fires that can use the firs as ladders to threaten mature Giant Sequoia crowns. Natural fires may also be important in keeping carpenter ants in check.

In 1970 the National Park Service began controlled burns of its groves to correct these problems. Current policies also allow natural fires to burn. One of these untamed burns severely damaged the second-largest tree in the world, the Washington tree, in September 2003, 45 days after the fire started. This damage made it unable to withstand the snowstorm of January 2005, leading to the collapse of over half the trunk.

In addition to fire, there are also two animal agents for Giant Sequoia seed release. The more significant of the two is a longhorn beetle (*Phymatodes nitidus*) that lays eggs on the cones, into which the larvae then bore holes. This cuts the vascular water supply to the cone scales, allowing the cones to dry and open for the seeds to fall. Cones damaged by the beetles during the summer will slowly open over the next several months. Some research indicates that many cones, particularly higher in the crowns, may need to be partially dried by beetle damage before fire can fully open them. The other agent is the Douglas Squirrel (*Tamiasciurus douglasi*) that gnaws on the fleshy green scales of younger cones. The squirrels are active year round, and some seeds are dislodged and dropped as the cone is eaten.

Discovery and Naming

The Giant Sequoia was well known to Native American tribes living in its area. Native American names for the species include Wawona, Toos-pung-ish and Hea-mi-withic, the latter two in the language of the Tule River Tribe.

The first reference to the Giant Sequoia by Europeans is in 1833, in the diary of the explorer J. K. Leonard; the reference does not mention any locality, but his route would have taken him through the Calaveras Grove. This discovery was not publicized. The next European to see the species was John M. Wooster, who carved his initials in the bark of the 'Hercules' tree in the Calaveras Grove in 1850; again, this received no publicity. Much more publicity was given to the "discovery" by Augustus T. Dowd of the Calaveras Grove in 1852, and this is commonly cited as the species' discovery. The tree found by Dowd, christened the 'Discovery Tree', was felled in 1853.

The first scientific naming of the species was by John Lindley in 1853, who named it *Wellingtonia gigantea*, without realizing this was an invalid name under the botanical code as the name *Wellingtonia* had already been used earlier for another unrelated plant (*Wellingtonia arnottiana* in the family Sabiaceae). The name "Wellingtonia" has persisted in England as a common name, though is deprecated as cultural imperialism (R. Ornduff in Aune 1994). The following year, Joseph Decaisne transferred it to the same genus as the Coast Redwood, naming it *Sequoia gigantea*, but again this name was invalid, having been applied earlier (in 1847, by Endlicher) to the Coast Redwood. The name *Washingtonia californica* was also applied to it by Winslow in 1854, though this too is invalid, belonging to the palm genus *Washingtonia*.

In 1907 it was placed by Carl Ernst Otto Kuntze in the otherwise fossil genus *Steinhauera,* but doubt as to whether the Giant Sequoia is related to the fossil originally so named makes this name invalid.

The nomenclatural oversights were finally corrected in 1939 by J. Buchholz, who also pointed out that the Giant Sequoia is distinct from the Coast Redwood at the genus level and coined the name *Sequoiadendron giganteum* for it.

Uses

Wood from mature Giant Sequoias is highly resistant to decay, but is fibrous and brittle, making it generally unsuitable for construction. From the 1880s through the 1920s logging took place in many groves in spite of marginal commercial returns. Due to their weight and brittleness trees would often shatter when they hit the ground, wasting much of the wood. Loggers attempted to cushion the impact by digging trenches and filling them with branches. Still, it is estimated that as little as 50 percent of the timber made it from groves to the mill. The wood was used mainly for shingles and fence posts, or even for matchsticks.

Pictures of the once majestic trees broken and abandoned in formerly pristine groves, and the thought of the giants put to such modest use, spurred the public outcry that caused most of the groves to be preserved as protected land. The public can visit an example of 1880s clear-cutting at Big Stump Grove near Grant Grove. As late as the 1980s some immature trees were logged in Sequoia National Forest, publicity of which helped lead to the creation of Giant Sequoia National Monument.

The wood from immature trees is less brittle, with recent tests on young plantation-grown trees showing it similar to Coast Redwood wood in quality. This is resulting in some interest in cultivating Giant Sequoia as a very high-yielding timber crop tree, both in California and also in parts of western Europe, where it may grow more efficiently than Coast Redwoods. In the northwest United States some entrepreneurs have also begun growing Giant Sequoias for Christmas trees. Besides these attempts at tree farming, the principal economic uses for Giant Sequoia today are tourism and horticulture.

Cultivation

Giant Sequoia is a very popular ornamental tree in many areas. Areas where it is successfully grown include most of western and southern Europe, the Pacific Northwest of North America north to southwest British Columbia, southeast Australia, New Zealand and central-southern Chile. It is also grown, though less successfully, in parts of eastern North America.

Sequoiadendron has been successfully planted in the British Isles, parts of continental Europe, as well as in much of the western, southern, and eastern USA. Trees can withstand temperatures of -31 °C (-25 °F) or colder, for short periods of time providing the ground around the roots is insulated with either heavy snow or mulch. Outside its natural range, sequoia's foliage suffers from damaging windburn. Large specimen examples grow in arboretums in Pennsylvania and Rhode Island USA. A large sequoia, planted by horticulturist Claude Heit in the 1960s, is growing in the Finger Lakes region of New York USA. An experimental private planting of young sequoia trees (less than 5 years old in early 2007) exists in Vermont USA. In Washington and Oregon, it is common to find giant sequoias that have been successfully planted in both urban and rural areas. In the Seattle area, large specimens (over 90 feet) are fairly common and exist in several city parks and many private yards (especially east Seattle including Capitol Hill, Washington Park, & Leschi/ Madrona). Additionally, Coast Redwoods can be seen in Lincoln Park and on the University of Washington campus.

The limit of winter cold tolerance is generally down to about -30 °C, but with a few individuals known to have tolerated lower temperatures, particularly where they benefit from deep snow cover over the roots.

Since its discovery a wide range of horticultural varieties have been selected, especially in Europe. There are, amongst others, weeping, variegated, pygmy, blue, grass green, and compact forms.

Europe

It was first brought into cultivation in 1853 by Scotsman John D. Matthew, who collected a small quantity of seed in the Calaveras Grove, arriving with it in Scotland in August 1853. A much larger shipment of seed collected (also in the Calaveras Grove) by William Lobb, acting for the Veitch Nursery at Budlake near Exeter, arrived in England in December 1853; seed from this batch was widely distributed throughout Europe.

Growth in Britain is very fast, with the tallest tree, at Benmore in southwest Scotland, reaching 54 m (177 ft) at age 150 years and several others from 50-53 m tall; the stoutest is around 12 m in girth and 4 m in diameter, in Perthshire. The Royal Botanic Gardens at Kew in London also contains a large specimen.

Growth rates in some areas are remarkable; one young tree in Italy reached 22 m (72.18 ft) tall and 88 cm (2.89 ft) trunk diameter in 17 years. Giant sequoias have also been planted in Belgium, the Netherlands and Luxembourg. The stoutest one has a diameter of 2.83 m (9.28 ft). Growth further northeast in Europe is limited by winter cold. In Denmark, where extreme winters can reach -32 □C, the largest tree was 35 m (114.83 ft) tall and 1.7 m (5.58 ft) diameter in 1976 and is bigger today. One in Poland has purportedly survived temperatures down to -37 °C with heavy snow cover.

USA and Canada

It is very successful in the Pacific Northwest from western Oregon north to southwest British Columbia, with fast growth rates.

In the northeastern USA there has been some limited success in growing the species, but growth is much slower there, and it is prone to *Cercospora* and *Kabatina* fungal diseases due to the hot, humid summer climate there. A tree at Blithewold Gardens, in Bristol, Rhode Island is reported to be 27 metres (90 ft) tall, reportedly the tallest in the New England states . The tree at the Tyler Arboretum in Delaware County, Pennsylvania at 29.1 m (95.4 ft) may be the tallest in the northeast. Specimens also grow in the Arnold Arboretum in Boston, Massachusetts (planted 1972, 18 m tall in 1998), at the Longwood Gardens near Wilmington, Delaware, and in the Finger Lakes region of New York for many years. Private plantings of Giant Sequoias around the Middle Atlantic States are not uncommon. Since 2000, a small amateur experimental planting has been underway in the Lake Champlain valley of Vermont at the Vermont Experimental Cold-Hardy Cactus Garden where winter temperatures can reach -37 □C with variable snowcover.

A cold-tolerant cultivar 'Hazel Smith' selected in about 1960 is proving more successful in the northeastern U.S.A. This clone was the sole survivor of several hundred seedlings grown at a nursery in New Jersey.

Australia

The Ballarat Botanical Gardens contain a significant collection, many of them about 150 years old. Also Jubilee Park in Daylesford. Cook Park in Orange, New South Wales also has a single specimen planted in about 1870.

New Zealand

Several impressive specimens of Sequoiadendron giganteum exist throughout the South Island of New Zealand. Notable examples include a set of trees in a public park of Picton, as well as robust specimens in the public and botanical parks of Queenstown.

THUJA PLICATA

Western redcedar (*Thuja plicata*) is a species of *Thuja*, an evergreen coniferous tree in the cypress family Cupressaceae, native to the northwestern United States and southwestern Canada, from southern Alaska and British Columbia south to northwest California and inland to western Montana. It is one of two arborvitaes native to North America; not a true cedar (Cedrus), but is the source of what are called cedar shingles.

Description

The foliage forms flat sprays with scale-like leaves in opposite pairs, with successive pairs at 90 to each other. The foliage sprays are green above, and green marked white with stomatal bands below. The cones are slender, 15-20 mm long and 4-5 mm broad, with 8-12 thin, overlapping scales.

Western redcedar is a large tree, to 55-75 m tall and 3 m (exceptionally 7 m) trunk diameter. The *Quinault Lake redcedar* (left) is the largest known western redcedar in the world with a wood volume of 500 cubic metres (17,700 cu ft). By way of comparison, the largest known tree, a Giant Sequoia named *General Sherman,* has a volume of 1,480 cubic metres (52,300 cu ft). Located near the northwest shore of Lake Quinault north of Aberdeen, Washington, about 34 km from the Pacific Ocean, the *Quinault Lake redcedar* is 55.0 m high with a diameter of 6.04 m (Van Pelt, 2002). A redcedar over 74 m tall and 800 years old stood in Cathedral Grove on Vancouver Island, British Columbia, before it was set on fire and destroyed by vandals in 1972.

It is among the most widespread trees in the Pacific Northwest, and is associated with Douglas-fir and western hemlock in most places where it grows. In addition to growing in lush forests, western redcedar is also a riparian tree, and grows in many forested swamps and streambanks in its range. The tree is shade-tolerant, and able to reproduce under dense shade.

Western redcedar is the Provincial tree of British Columbia. It is also known (mainly in the American horticultural trade) as Giant Arborvitae. The name western redcedar is also sometimes split into three words as 'Western Red Cedar', though this can cause confusion, as it is not a cedar.

Uses

The soft red-brown timber is valued for its resistance to decay, being extensively used for outdoor construction in the form of posts, decking, shingles, siding, and so forth. It is cultivated as an ornamental tree and also (to a limited extent) in forestry plantations and for screens and hedges. It has been introduced to other parts of the temperate zone, including western Europe, Australia (at least as far north as Sydney), New Zealand, the eastern United States and higher elevations of Hawaii. It is also used to line closets and chests, for its pungent aromatic oils are believed to discourage moth and carpet beetle larvae, which can damage cloth by eating wool and similar fibers. This is of course more effective in a properly constructed *redcedar chest* (sometimes made entirely of cedar), since the oils are confined by shellac and leather seals. A well-sealed redcedar chest will retain its pungent odor for many decades, sometimes for over a century. Its light weight and strength make it a popular choice for guitar soundboards.

Indigenous Peoples Uses

Western redcedar has an extensive history of use by the indigenous people of the northwest coast of North America, from Oregon to southeast Alaska . Some northwest coast tribes refer to themselves as "people of the redcedar" because of their extensive dependence on the tree for basic materials . Red cedar wood is used to make huge monoxyle canoes in which the men went out to high sea to harpoon whales , totem poles, houses, masks, helmets, armor, boxes, utensils, tools, and many other art and utility objects.

One of those canoes (a 38 feet craft dug out about a century ago) , was bought in 1901 by Captain John Voss , an adventurer . He gave her the name of Tilikum (boat) ("Friend" in Chinook jargon), rigged her , and led her in a three years hectic voyage from British Columbia to London (G.B.).

Bark

The bark is easily removed from live trees in long strips, and is harvested for use in making mats, rope and cordage, basketry, rain hats, clothing, and other soft goods. The harvesting of bark must be done with care because if the tree is completely stripped it will die. To prevent this, the harvester only harvests from trees which have not been stripped before, and usually less than a half round of the bark is removed. After harvesting the tree is not used for bark again, although it may later be felled for wood. Stripping bark is usually started with a series of cuts at the base of the tree above any buttresses, and the bark is peeled upwards. To remove bark high up, a pair of platforms strung on rope around the tree are used, and the harvester climbs by alternating between them for support. Since redcedars lose their lower branches as all tall trees do in the rainforest, the harvester may climb 10 m or more into the tree by this method. The harvested bark is folded and carried in backpacks. It can be stored for quite some time as mold does not grow on it, and is moistened before unfolding and working. It is then split lengthwise into the required width and woven or twisted into shape. Bark harvesting was mostly done by women, despite the danger of climbing 10 m in the air, because they were the primary makers of bark goods. Today bark rope making is a lost art in many communities, although it is still practiced for decoration or art in a few places. Other uses of bark are still common for artistic or practical purposes.

Wood

Redcedar branches are very flexible and have good tensile strength. They were stripped and used as strong cords for fishing line, rope cores, twine, and other purposes where bark cord was not strong enough or might fray. Both the branches and bark rope have been replaced by modern fiber and nylon cordage among the aboriginal northwest coast peoples, though the bark is still in use for the other purposes mentioned above.

Harvesting redcedars required some ceremony, and included propitiation of the tree's spirits as well as those of the surrounding trees. In particular, many people specifically requested the tree and its brethren not to fall or drop heavy branches on the harvester, a situation which is mentioned in a number of different stories of people who were not sufficiently careful. Some professional loggers of Native American descent have mentioned that they offer quiet or silent propitiations to trees which they fell, following in this tradition.

Felling of large trees such as redcedar before the introduction of steel tools was a complex and time-consuming art. Typically the bark was removed around the base of the tree above the buttresses, and then some amount of cutting and splitting with stone adzes and mauls would be done, creating a wide triangular cut. The area above and below the cut would be covered with a mixture of wet moss and clay as a firebreak, and then the cut would be packed with tinder and small kindling and slowly burned. The process of cutting and burning would alternate until the tree was mostly penetrated through, and then careful tending of the fire would fell the tree in the best direction for handling. This process could take many days, and constant rotation of workers was involved to keep the fires burning through night and day, often in a remote and forbidding location. Once the tree was felled the work had only just begun, as it then had to be stripped and dragged down to shore. If the tree was to become canoes then it would often be divided into sections and worked into rough canoe shapes before transport, but if it were to be used for a totem pole or building materials it would be towed in the round to the village. Many trees are still felled in this traditional manner for use as totem poles and canoes, particularly by artists who feel that using modern tools is detrimental to the traditional spirit of the art. Non-traditionalists simply buy redcedar logs or lumber at mills or lumber yards, a practice that is commonly followed by most working in smaller sizes such as for masks and staves.

Because felling required such an extraordinary amount of work, if only planks for housing were needed, these would be split from the living tree. The bark was stripped and saved, and two cuts were made at the ends of the planking. Then wedges would be pounded in along the sides and the planks slowly split off the side of the tree. Trees which have been so harvested are still visible in some places in the rainforest, with obvious chunks taken off of their sides. Such trees usually continue to grow perfectly well, since redcedar wood is resistant to decay.

AGATHIS AUSTRALIS

Agathis australis, commonly known as the kauri, is a coniferous tree found north of 38°S in the northern districts of New Zealand's North Island. It is the largest (by volume) but not tallest species of tree in the country, standing up to 50m tall in the emergent layer above the forest's main canopy. The tree has smooth bark and small oval leaves. Other common names to distinguish *A. australis* from other members of the genus are southern kauri and New Zealand kauri.

Though kauri are among the most ancient trees in the world, they have developed a unique niche in the forest. With their novel soil interaction and regeneration pattern they are able to compete with the more recently evolved and faster growing angiosperms. Because it is such a conspicuous species, forest containing kauri is generally known as kauri forest, though kauri need not be the most abundant tree. In the warmer northern climate, kauri forests have a higher species richness than others found further south.

Description

Young plants grow straight upwards and have the form of a narrow cone with branches going out along the length of the trunk. However, as they gain in height, the lowest branches are shed, preventing epiphytes from climbing. By maturity, the top branches form an imposing crown that stand out over all other native trees, dominating the heights of the forest.

The flaking bark of the kauri tree defends it from parasitic plants, and accumulates around the base of the trunk. On large trees it may pile up to a height of 2 m or more. The kauri has a habit of forming small clumps or patches scattered through mixed forests

Kauri leaves are 3 to 7 cm long and 1 cm broad, tough and leathery in texture, with no midrib; they are arranged in opposite pairs or whorls of three on the stem. The seed cones are globose, 5 to 7 cm diameter, and mature 18 to 20 months after pollination; the seed cones disintegrate at maturity to release winged seeds, which are then dispersed by the wind. While the reproduction of kauri seed cones takes place between male and female seed cones of the same tree, fertilisation of the seeds occurs by pollination, which may be driven by the same or another tree's pollen. Kauri forests are among the most ancient in the world. The antecedents of the kauri appeared during the Jurassic period (between 190 and 135 million years).

Size

Agathis australis can attain heights of 40 to 50 metres and trunk diameters big enough to rival Californian Sequoias at over 5 meters. The largest kauris do not attain as much height or girth at ground level but contain more timber in their cylindrical trunks than a comparable Sequoia with its tapering stem. The largest specimen of which there is any known record grew on the mountains at the head of the Tararu Creek that falls into the Hauraki Gulf just north of the mouth of the Waihou River (Thames). This tree was known as The Great Ghost. Local Thames Historian Alastair Isdale noted this tree was 8.54 metres in diameter, and 26.83 metres in girth. It was consumed by fire c.1890.

A kauri tree at Mill Creek, Mercury Bay was measured in the early 1840s to be 22 metres in circumference and 24 metres to the first branches. It is thought that this tree was felled around 1870.

Growth Rate and Age

In general over the lifetime of the tree the growth rate tends to increase, reach a maximum, then decline. A 1987 study measured mean annual diameter increments ranging from 1.5 to 4.6 mm per year with an overall average of 2.3 mm per year. This is equivalent to 8.7 annual rings per centimetre of core, said to be half the commonly quoted figure for growth rate. The same study concluded only a weak relationship between age and diameter. Individuals in the same 10 cm diameter class may vary in age by 300 years, and the largest individual on any particular site is often not the oldest. Experts agree that because of the variation in growth rate it is not possible to accurately assess the age of a standing tree from its diameter alone. Trees can normally live longer than 600 years. Probably many individuals exceed 1000 years, but there is no conclusive evidence that trees can exceed 2000 years in age. (Ahmed & Ogden 1987).

Root Structure and Soil Interaction

One of the defining aspects of this tree's unique niche is its relationship with the soil below. Much like podocarps, it feeds in the organic litter near the surface of the soil through fine root hairs. This layer of the soil is composed of organic matter derived from falling leaves and branches as well as dead trees, and is constantly undergoing decomposition. On the other hand, broadleaf trees such as Mahoe derive a good fraction of their nutrition in the deeper mineral layer of the soil. Although its root system is very shallow, it also has several downwardly directed *peg roots* which anchor it firmly in the soil. Such a solid foundation is necessary for a tree the size of a kauri to avoid blowing over, especially during storms and cyclones.

The litter left by kauri is much more acidic than most trees, and as it decays similarly acidic compounds are liberated. In a process known as leaching, these acidic molecules pass through the soil layers with the help of rainfall, and release other nutrients trapped in clay such as nitrogen and phosphorus. This leaves these important nutrients unavailable to other trees, as they are washed down into deeper layers. This process is known as podsolization, and changes the soil colour to a dull grey. For a single tree, this leaves an area of leached soil beneath known as a *cup podsol*. This leaching process is important for kauri's survival as it competes with other species for space. eaf litter and other decaying parts of a kauri decompose much slower than most other species, however. Besides its acidity, the plant also bears substances such as waxes and phenols that are harmful to microorganisms. This results in a large buildup of litter around the base of a mature tree, in which its own roots feed. These feeding roots also house a symbiotic fungi known as mycorrhiza which increase the plant's efficiency in taking up nutrients. In this mutualistic relationship, the fungus derives its own nutrition from the roots. In its interactions with the soil kauri is thus able to starve its competitors of much needed nutrients and compete with much younger lineages.

Distributions

Local Spatial Distribution

In terms of local topography, kauri is far from randomly dispersed. As mentioned above, kauri relies on depriving its competitors of nutrition in order to survive. However, one important consideration not discussed thus far is the slope of the land. Water on hills flows downward by the action of gravity, taking with in nutrients in the soil. This results in a gradient from nutrient poor soil at the top of slopes to nutrient rich soils below. As nutrients leached are replaced by aqueous nitrates and phosphates from above, kauri trees are less able to inhibit the growth of strong competitors such as angiosperms. In contrast, the leaching process is only enhanced on higher elevation. In Waipoua Forest this is reflected in higher abundances of kauri on ridge crests, and greater concentrations of its main competitors, such as taraire are found at low elevations. This pattern is known as niche partitioning, and allows more than one species to occupy the same area. Those species which live alongside kauri include tawari, a montane broadleaf tree which is normally found in higher altitudes, where nutrient cycling is naturally slow.

Changes Over Geological Time

Kauri is presently found north of 38□S latitude, its southern limit stretching from Kawhia Harbour in the west to the eastern Kaimai Range. However, its distribution has changed greatly over geological time due to the phenomenon of climate change. This is exemplified in the recent Holocene epoch by migration southwards following the peak of the last Ice Age. During this time when frozen ice sheets covered much of the world's continents, kauri was able to survive only in isolated pockets, its main refuge being in the very far north. Radiocarbon dating is one technique used by scientists to uncover the history of this tree's distribution, with stump kauri from peat swamps being used for measurement. The coldest period in recent time occurred very roughly 15-20,000 years ago, and during this time kauri was apparently confined north of Kaitaia, which itself is not far from the northern most point of the North Island, North Cape. Much like kumaras grown in New Zealand, kauri requires a mean temperature of 17°C or more for the majority of the year. Kauri's retreat can in fact be used as a proxy for temperature changes during this period.

It remains unclear whether kauri recolonized the North Island from a single refuge in the far north or from scattered pockets of isolated stands that managed to survive despite climatic conditions. It spread south through Whangarei, past Dargaville and as far south as Waikato, attaining its peak distribution during the years 3000-2000 BP There is some suggestion it has receded somewhat since then, which may indicate temperatures have declined slightly since this time.

During the peak of its movement southwards, it was traveling as fast as 200 metres per year. Regardless of where it originated from, its spread southward seems relatively rapid for a tree that can take a millennium to reach complete maturity. This can be explained by its life history pattern.

Kauri relies on wind as its means of both pollination and seed dispersal, whereas many other natives may have their seeds carried large distances by frugivores (animals which eat fruit) such as the kereru, a native pigeon. However, kauri trees rapidly reach a stage at which they can produce seeds, taking only 50 years or so before giving rise to their own offspring. This trait makes them somewhat like a pioneer species, despite the fact that their long lifespan is characteristic of k-selected species.

Just as the niche of kauri is differentiated through its interactions with the soil, it also has a separate regeneration 'strategy' compared to its broadleaf neighbours. The relationship is very similar to the podocarp-broadleaf forests further south; kauri is much more light demanding and requires larger gaps to regenerate, whereas broadleaf trees such as puriri and kohekohe show far more shade tolerance. These species can regenerate in areas where lower levels of light reach ground level, for example from a single branch falling off. Kauri trees must therefore remain alive long enough for a large disturbance to occur, allowing them sufficient light to regenerate. In areas where large amounts of forest are destroyed, such as by logging, kauri seedlings are able to regenerate much easier due not only to increased sunlight, but their stronger resistance to wind and frosts. Kauri resides in the emergent layer of the forest, where it is exposed to the effects of the weather, however smaller trees that dominate the main canopy are sheltered both by the emergent trees above and by each other. Left in open areas without protection they are far less capable of regenerating.

Due to this special regeneration niche, kauri trees can live over a thousand years, whereas most other trees experience senescence long before this time. This extraordinary age is simply a reflection of how long this species must wait in order for there to be a disturbance large enough to favour its regeneration. The nature of this large disturbance also means that kauri trees regenerate *en mass*, resulting in a *cohort* or generation of trees of similar ages forming after each disturbance. Kauri in a given area are hence likely to be of similar age. Due to the nature of their regeneration, the distribution of kauri allows researchers to predict when and where disturbances have occurred, and how large they may have been; the presence of abundant kauri may be an indication that an area is prone to disturbances. Kauri seedlings still occur in areas with low light, of course, but mortality rates for such seedlings are much higher, and those that survive self thinning and grow to sapling stage tend to be found in higher light environments.

During periods with less disturbances kauri tends to lose ground to broadleaf competitors which are more capable of establishing themselves in shaded environments. In the complete absence of disturbance, kauri tends to become more rare as it is excluded by its competitors. Biomass of kauri tends to decrease during such times, as more biomass becomes concentrated in angiosperm species like towai. Kauri trees also tend to become more randomly distributed in terms of their age, with each tree dying at a different point in time, and regeneration gaps being rare and sporadic. Over thousands of years these varying regeneration strategies produce a 'tug of war' effect where kauri retreats uphill during periods of calm, then takes over lower areas briefly during mass disturbances. Although such trends are impossible to observe in the lifetime of a human, research into current patterns of distribution, behavior of species in experimental conditions, and study of pollen sediments (see palynology) have helped shed light on the life history of kauri.

Deforestation

Heavy logging which began around 1820 and continued for a century has considerably decreased the number of kauri trees in New Zealand It has been estimated that prior to European colonisation, the kauri forests of northern New Zealand occupied at least 12,000 square kilometres. By the 1950s this area had decreased to about 1,400 km², comprising some 47 forests which were depleted of their best kauri. By 1900, less than 10% of the original kauri had survived. It is estimated that today, there is 4% of uncut forest left in small pockets.

Estimates are that around half of the timber had been accidentally or wilfully burnt. More than half of the remainder had been exported to Australia, Britain, and other countries, while the balance was used locally for building houses and ships. Much of the timber was sold for a return sufficient only to cover wages and expenses, plus reasonable interest on the capital employed in the industry. From 1871 to 1895 the receipts indicate a rate of about 8 shillings (around NZD$20 in 2003) per hundred superficial feet (34 shillings/m³).

The Government continued to sell large areas of kauri forests to sawmillers who, under no restrictions, took the most effective and economical steps to secure the timber, resulting in much waste and destruction. At one sale in 1908 more than five thousand standing kauris, totalling about twenty million superficial feet (47,000 m³), were sold for less than two pounds per tree (two pounds in 1908 equates to around NZD$100 in 2003 It is said that in 1890 the royalty on standing timber fell in some cases to as low as twopence (NZD$0.45 in 2003) per hundred superficial feet (8 pence/m³), though the expense of cutting and removing it to the mills was typically great due to the difficult terrain they were located in.

Uses

Although today their use is far more restricted, in the past the size and strength of kauri timber made it a popular wood for construction and ship building, particularly for masts of sailing ships due to its parallel grain and the absence of branches extending for much of its height. Kauri crown and stump (tree) wood was much appreciated for its beauty, and was sought after for ornamental wood panelling as well as high-end furniture. Though not as highly prized, the light colour of kauri trunk wood made it also well-suited for more utilitarian furniture construction, as well as for use in the fabrication of cisterns, barrels, bridges construction material, fences, moulds for metal forges, large rollers for the textile industry, railroad ties and braces for mines and tunnels, among many others.

In the late nineteenth and early twentieth centuries kauri gum (semi-fossilised kauri resin) was a valuable commodity, particularly for varnish, and was the focus of a considerable industry at the time.

Timber

Technical specifications

- Moisture content of dried wood: 12%
- Density of wood: 560 kg/m^3
- Tensile strength: 88 MPa
- Modulus of elasticity: 9.1 GPa
- After felled kauri wood dries to a 12% moisture content, the tangential contraction is 4.1% and the radial contraction is 2.3%

A considerable number of kauri have been found buried in what are today salt marshes, resulting from ancient natural changes such as volcanic eruptions, sea level changes and floods. Such trees have been radiocarbon dated to originating as far back as 50,000 years ago or older. The bark and the seed cones of the trees often survive together with the trunk, although when excavated and in contact with the air, these parts display rapid deterioration.

The quality of the disinterred wood varies, and some is in surprisingly good shape, comparable to that of newly-felled kauri, although often lighter in colour. This aspect can be improved by the use of natural dyes, which provide brown dark and greenish tones that heighten the details of the grain. After a drying process, such ancient kauri can still be made use of for furniture and other construction.

Conservation and Kauri Today

The small remaining pockets of kauri forest in New Zealand have survived in areas that were not subjected to burning by Maori settlers and were too inaccessible to European loggers. The largest area of mature kauri forest is Waipoua Forest in Northland. Mature and regenerating kauri can also be found in other National and Regional Parks such as Puketi and Omahutà Forests in Northland, the Waitakere Ranges near Auckland, and Coromandel Forest Park on the Coromandel Peninsula.

The importance of Waipoua Forest in relation to the kauri was that it remained the only kauri forest retaining its former virgin condition, and that it was extensive enough to give reasonable promise of permanent survival. On 2 July 1952 an area of over 80 km^2 of Waipoua was proclaimed a forest sanctuary after a petition to the Government. It contains three quarters of New Zealand's remaining kauri.

In 1921 a philanthropic Cornishman named James Trounson sold to the Government for 40 thousand pounds, a large area adjacent to a few acres of crown land and said to contain at least four thousand kauris. From time to time Trounson had added further areas by way of gift, until what is known as Trounson Park comprised a total of 4 km^2.

The most famous specimens are *Tane Mahuta* and *Te Matua Ngahere* in Waipoua Forest. These two trees have become tourist attractions due to their size. Tane Mahuta, named after the Maori forest god, is the biggest existing kauri with a girth of 13.77 m (45.2 ft), a trunk height of 17.68 m (58.0 ft), a total height of 51.2 m (168 ft)[15] and a total volume including the crown of 516.7 m^3 (18,247 cu ft)

Kauri is common as a specimen tree in parks and gardens throughout New Zealand, prized for the distinctive look of young trees, its low maintenance once established (though seedlings are frost tender), and small footprint.

In the 1970s, kauri dieback caused by a phytophthora was discovered on Great Barrier Island. The disease, known as kauri collar rot, has since started spreading through kauri forests on the mainland The disease causes yellowing leaves, thinning canopy, dead branches, lesions that bleed resin and tree death. It is caused by *Phytophthora* taxon *Agathis* (PTA) which was identified as a new species in April 2008. Its closest known relative is *Phytophthora katsurae* The phytophthora is believed to be spread on people's shoes or by mammals, particularly feral pigs.

NORWAY SPRUCE

Norway Spruce (*Picea abies*) is a species of spruce native to Europ. It is a large evergreen coniferous tree growing to 35-55 m tall ad with a trunk diameter of up to 1-1.5 m. The shoots areorange-brown and glabrous (hairless). The leaves are needle-like, 1-24 mm long, quadrangular in cross-section (not flattened), and dark green on all four sides with inconspicuous stomatal lines. The cones are 9-17 cm long (the longest of any spruce), and have bluntly to sharply triangular-pointed scale tips. They are green or reddish, maturing brown 5-7 months after pollination. The seeds are black, 4-5 mm long, with a pale brown 15 mm wing.

The Norway Spruce grows throughout northeast Europe from Norway and Poland eastward, and also in the mountains of central Europe, southwest to the western end of the Alps, and southeast in the Carpathians and Balkans to the extreme north of Greece. The northern limit is in the arctic, just north of 70□N in Norway. Its eastern limit in Russia is hard to define, due to extensive hybridisation and intergradation with the Siberian Spruce (*Picea obovata*, syn. *P. abies* subsp. *obovata*), but is usually given as the Ural Mountains. However, trees showing some Siberian Spruce characters extend as far west as much of northern Finland, with a few records in northeast Norway. The hybrid is known as *Picea x fennica* (or *P.* □ subsp. *fennica*, if the two taxa are considered subspecies), and can be distinguished by a tendency towards having hairy shoots and cones with smoothly rounded scales.

Populations in southeast Europe tend to have on average longer cones with more pointed scales; these are sometimes distinguished as *Picea abies* var. *acuminata* (Beck) Dallim. & A.B.Jacks., but there is extensive overlap in variation with trees from other parts of the range.

Some botanists treat Siberian Spruce as a subspecies of Norway Spruce, though in their typical forms, they are very distinct, the Siberian Spruce having cones only 5-10 cm long, with smoothly rounded scales, and pubescent (hairy) shoots. Genetically Norway and Siberian Spruces have turned out to be extremely similar and should be considered as two closely related subspecies of *P. abies*.

Another spruce with smoothly rounded cone scales and hairy shoots occurs rarely in the central Alps in eastern Switzerland. It is also distinct in having thicker, blue-green leaves. Many texts treat this as a variant of Norway Spruce, but it is as distinct as many other spruces, and appears to be more closely related to Siberian Spruce, Schrenk's Spruce (*P. schrenkiana*) from central Asia and Morinda Spruce (*P. smithiana*) in the Himalaya. Treated as a distinct species, it takes the name Alpine Spruce (*Picea alpestris* (Brügger) Stein). As with Siberian Spruce, it hybridises extensively with Norway Spruce; pure specimens are rare.

A press release from Umeå University says that a Norway Spruce clone named Old Tjikko, carbon dated as 9,550 years old, is the "oldest living tree." However, Pando, a Quaking Aspen clone, is estimated to be between 80,000 and one million years old The oldest known individual tree is Methuselah, a Great Basin Bristlecone Pine.

Uses

Norway Spruce is one of the most widely planted spruces, both in and outside of its native range, used in forestry for timber and paper production, and as an ornamental tree in parks and gardens. It is also widely planted for use as a Christmas tree. Every Christmas, the Norwegian capital city of Oslo provides the cities of New York, London, Edinburgh and Washington D.C. with a Norwegian spruce, which is placed at the most central square of each city. This is mainly a sign of gratitude for the aid these countries gave during the Second World War.

It is naturalised in some parts of North America, though not so extensively as to be considered an invasive weed tree. It can grow fast when young, up to 1 m per year for the first 25 years under good conditions, but becomes slower once over around 20 m tall. Several cultivars have been selected for garden use.

3

TREE RINGS

INTRODUCTION

The main parts of the tree are the leaves, the trunk and the roots. Each plays an important part in the growth and vitality of the tree. Trees grow bigger each year from two places: the buds and the cambium.

Buds

Most of the buds that grow on a tree are at the tips of branches and roots. From these, branches and roots grow longer each year, and produce new branches and roots. Trees also have adventitious buds in the bark along branches and roots. These buds lie dormant until the tree needs them. Sprouts from adventitious buds help a tree stay alive after a catastrophe where the tree looses the end of its branches (during a storm, for example, or after topping). These sprouts are weakly attached to the tree and generally undesirable, but they do play a role in the life of many trees.

Cambium

All woody plants have an actively growing layer of cells, called the cambium, that lies between the bark and the wood of the trunk and branches. From the cambium, the tree puts on a new layer of wood each year. This layer, or "ring," covers over the old layers on the trunk, branches and woody roots of the tree.

Use your fingernail to scrape some bark off a twig at any time of year. The green layer you see is the cambium. Use care! The place that you scrape is a wound that the tree will have to repair.

Some trees, like maples, do not naturally form heartwood. When wounds cause maple trees to defend themselves against decay, they form dark colored wood called wound-induced heartwood.

Leaves

Trees produce all the food they need in their leaves. Through a process called photosynthesis, leaves use the green pigment chlorophyll, along with light energy from the sun, to turn carbon dioxide and water into sugar. The trees use sugar for energy and to produce wood. Through this process, trees take carbon dioxide (a pollutant) out of the air and turn it into oxygen and wood.

In the process called transpiration, trees move water solutions throughout the tree. To keep themselves cool, leaves release water vapor through pores. This keeps the area around the tree cool, too.

Trunk and Branches

These woody parts provide support for leaves and other branches. They are pathways for the movement of substances within the tree. The outer rings of wood are sapwood. Water moves up the tree through vessels in sapwood. Trees use wood in branches and in the trunk to store food for later use. Heartwood is the central, usually darker, less-active portion of a tree. Bark protects the cambium from harm like insulation and siding on a house protect it from rain, wind and cold. Food moves down the tree through the inner bark.

Roots

Large woody roots anchor the tree in the ground and store starch. They are a pathway for the movement of substances in the tree. From the soil, tiny absorbing roots take up water and minerals. These are carried up into the tree through woody roots.

Trees shed small roots and produce new ones each year just as they do with leaves. Roots grow throughout the year, especially in the early spring and in the fall.

Roots may have a beneficial relationship with fungi called mycorrhizae. The fungus extends from the tiniest tree roots out into the soil to help the tree absorb water and nutrients. The tree provides the fungus with food and a place to live.

Trees go through annual cycles of growth. Roots are busy in the early spring and late fall. Leaves and twigs grow in spring and the tree adds wood all summer long.

Tree wounds never heal. The best the tree can do is grow over wounds and seal them off. Anything that breaks through the bark of a tree causes a wound.

Trees produce much more oxygen then they use. They use carbon dioxide and produce oxygen during photosynthesis. They use oxygen during respiration. Trees and other plants produce the oxygen humans breath - thanks trees!

What Trees Need Light

Light from the sun provides the energy trees need to manufacture food.

Water

Trees need water to prevent wilting, produce food, move substances throughout the tree and for cooling.

Nutrients

Trees need 16 elements to grow. They get carbon and oxygen from air, hydrogen and oxygen from water, and everything else from soil. They need lots of nitrogen, phosphorus and potassium, and lesser amounts of sulphur, calcium and magnesium. They need a little bit of boron, chlorine, copper, iron, manganese, molybdenum and zinc.

Room To Grow

Tree roots need plenty of room to grow so they can anchor the tree, and take up water and minerals. Branches need room to spread and capture energy from the sun. Branches need space away from buildings, roadways, utility lines and other trees so they can grow to their natural size without injury or excessive pruning.

Well-Drained Soil

Trees need soil that drains and allows the free movement of oxygen, other gases and water. When soil pore spaces are full of water or are compacted, tree roots cannot get everything they need to function properly.

TREE TRUNKS

Tree trunks grow bigger each year when the cambium adds a new layer of wood over the old layers. The cambium produces large cells in the spring and smaller cells during the summer. In many trees the early cells are light in color and later cells are dark in color. Since the trunk of a tree is round, the result is a pattern that appears as rings. We call these annual rings or tree rings. Since trees generally produce one ring for each year of growth, you can find the age of a tree by counting its rings.

Find out which were good years and which were bad years by looking at the relative width of the rings. Can you tell which years had good rainfall, warm temperatures and few insect or disease outbreaks? The wider the growth ring, the better the growing conditions were that year.

The presence of covered-over wounds provides information about previous fires, insect or disease attacks, and when and where branches grew. If your tree once got hit by a lawn mower and its bark torn, there is a record of it in your tree. Careful inspection reveals the age of the tree when each of these events occurred.

URBAN ECOSYSTEMS

An ecosystem is a complex network of climate, soil, animals, microbes, plants and people. A lake, forest, prairie or watershed is an ecosystem. Although they are not natural, urban areas are ecosystems, too.

The vegetation in your community probably looks a lot different than the native forest or prairie that was there before European settlers came to Minnesota. Minnesota is an ecological transition zone where three distinctly different types of ecosystems meet: hardwood forest; coniferous (evergreen) forest; and prairie. Each ecosystem has climate, soils, plants, animals and microbes commonly associated with it. Each also has tree species which are adapted to its specific growing conditions.

Vegetation in an urban ecosystem has been altered by humans. As a result, urban areas typically have low species diversity, isolated groups of trees, poor nutrient cycling and confined rooting space. Add to these compacted and infertile soil, de-icing salts, pesticides, a lack of water and vandalism and the challenges that face plants in urban ecosystems seems insurmountable.

Rural ecosystems have their own share of seemingly insurmountable problems including fire, floods, drought and storms. Lakes fill in with vegetation over time, rivers change course. Over thousands of years, plants and animals have adapted and they survive. What is different in the urban ecosystem is that it is the activities of humans that have affected the order of things. It follows that it is the activities of humans that can restore the health of urban ecosystems.

In the urban ecosystem, humans need trees and trees need humans. Often our success in establishing trees, collectively called the urban forest, depends on our ability to imitate the conditions in which trees grow in their natural environment. We need to make trees feel at home.

If ecological health is a goal in our communities, we need to find ways to sustain a diverse population of trees and other plants. The first step is finding out what was natural in an area and what is left of it. Most natural resource managers consider the vegetation that was in an area prior to the 1850s as native to that area. You can find clues to what is native, such as very old trees or undisturbed soils, but to paint the whole picture, you need to do some research. In the section that follows is information that will help you research the vegetation on a site.

Here are a few ways to ensure the ecological health of the urban ecosystem:

- Preserve areas of native vegetation;
- Protect vegetation communities: trees with their companion shrubs, flowers and grasses;
- Plant trees that are native to an area.

GREEN HISTORY

With a little research, you can get an idea of what the vegetation was like on a site at some period in the past. For some types of projects, such as restoration of natural areas or historical sites, this is an essential step. For any project, understanding the vegetation history gives clues to what may or may not be successful in the future.

For restoration of natural areas, project planners usually want to know what was native to the site before European settlers arrived. Although affected by American Indian land management practices, especially the use of fire, our landscapes were not drastically altered until European settlers arrived and began logging and farming. Most of the landscape of Minnesota was altered by the mid 1900s.

Land alteration continues today. Urban sprawl threatens much of what remains of our natural plant and animal communities. Few places in Minnesota have not been farmed, logged, grazed, sodded or paved. If yours is a site with an intact native habitat, you have a special stewardship responsibility.

To do a quality job of restoring vegetation on a developed site requires research as well. These sites include historical parks and the grounds of buildings undergoing restoration. Each of these restorations should include a study of the vegetation present on the site as it is now, as it was originally designed, and at any other appropriate period of time. Restoration may require making some plant substitutions. European buckthorn was once used for hedges, but is now recognized as an inappropriate invasive exotic species that causes harm to natural areas.

Fortunately there are excellent resources available to guide you to an understanding of the green history of a site. Keep in mind that when we describe the vegetation on a site at a particular period of time, that it is like looking at a single frame on a film strip. It makes a fine snapshot, but you really just see part of the picture. Vegetation is not static. It is part of an ever changing system. In nature, plant communities go through stages of succession. In the absence of fire for example, oak savannah becomes an oak woodland. Oak woodland may become a forest of maple and basswood (linden) trees. When disaster strikes, the cycle repeats itself.

Look for green history information in books and atlases, in biological studies, historical records and on the land itself. For some areas there are published books on native habitats. You may find useful information on the internet. A person who studies genealogy (family history) as a hobby can direct you to sources of good local information. A forester or naturalist may be able to interpret the history of a site by looking at the site itself.

To begin your research of a site you need to know its legal description. The entire state of Minnesota is divided into townships, each six miles square. Within each township, there are 36 sections. Each section is a square, one mile on each side. Each township has a unique description that tells where it is located relative to a particular point on the globe.

To find the legal description of a site, look in a county plat book or at a United States Geological Survey (USGS) topographic map. Your local library, city hall, county extension office, Soil and Water Conservation District office or Department of Natural Resources Forestry office may have a copy of each of these maps. In the future, you may be able to find these maps through the internet. Between 1847 and 1907, the United States Surveyor General surveyed the entire state of Minnesota. Surveyors walked along section lines and marked each section corner. As they went, surveyors made notes about the topography, soil quality, plant cover and the other natural features of the landscape. These original surveyors field notes help researchers learn the pre-settlement vegetation of an area.

The Minnesota Historical Society has some (but not all) of these original surveyors field notes. To see them, visit the Weyerhaeuser Reference Room at the Minnesota History Center in downtown St. Paul. Ask the librarian to direct you to the index of government documents in the State Archives and look up the U.S. Surveyor General. In the index you will find the reference number that you need to request the surveyors notes for the township in which you are interested. The staff will bring the handwritten books from the archives to the Reference Room.

A complete set of U.S. Surveyor General field notes for Minnesota is in the custody of the Secretary of State. You can request a copy of the field notes for the section where your site is located. Send a letter including the section, township and range of your site to the Business Services Division of the Secretary of State's office. There is a per-page charge for the information.

The information that U.S. Surveyor General surveyors gathered was compiled and mapped in 1930 by Frances J. Marschner. The United States Department of Agriculture (USDA) Forest Service published the map in 1974. There is a simplified version of the map in the publication Natural Vegetation of Minnesota At the Time of the Public Land Survey, 1847- 1907, by the Minnesota Department of Natural Resources Natural Heritage Program.

The Natural Heritage Program is responsible for conducting research, taking assessment, and promoting wise stewardship of Minnesota's native flora. At the heart of the program is a database on information on the state's rare species and sensitive natural habitats. With the Nongame Wildlife program, they conduct the County Biological Survey, a systematic county-by county inventory of threatened natural habitats and rare plant and animal species. One of the most useful products of this effort are large maps of each completed county, including those in the Minneapolis and St. Paul metropolitan area. Each map shows what remains of the natural vegetation that was present at the time of the land survey. It also shows what vegetation was once natural throughout the county. To see if the County Biological Survey is complete for your area, visit the DNR web site.

Local history books often include descriptions of the landscape or contain clues such as photographs or timber harvesting information. Old atlases may be helpful, as are old postcards and other photographs. Some of these references are available at your local library or county historical society. The Minnesota History Center has atlases and plat books on microfilm or microfiche in the Ronald M. Hubbs Room.

To make wise decisions you need up to date information about your community and the trees that grow there. An inventory can give you the information you need. It is the basis for planning. Consider these examples:

- You want to plant street trees along Main Street. You do not know how many spaces are available, how big the spaces are or if overhead utility lines are a problem.
- You know that some trees in a park may not be safe, because you can see cracked and rotting branches in them, but you are not sure which are hazardous to people or property.
- You want to hire an arborist to prune the street trees in your town, but you do not know how much money you need to get the job done.

An inventory is a method of collecting and organizing information about trees. Use the information to plan for maximum public benefits at minimum expense. Before you conduct a tree inventory, decide what information you need to make decisions and manage trees. Once collected, inventory information becomes outdated quickly. For the best return on your investment, only collect information that you need. Without regular updates, an inventory has little value after about five years.

The first step is to gather whatever information already exists for your community. At city hall, ask for a copy of the city base map. If there is no base map available, a U.S. Geological Survey map will work. If the city has a plan (some cities do comprehensive planning), try to get a copy, especially of the maps. On a map, draw the landscape features of your community. Include parks, rivers, unique features, highways, streets, land use and so on. As you add features, a picture of your community emerges. You will see how your community fits into the surrounding landscape. Along with the tree inventory, the map can help you identify opportunities.

Once you define its objective, choose a type of inventory. To make a simple windshield survey, drive along each street and count the number of trees and the number of empty tree planting spaces. For a detailed, state-of-the-art inventory, hire a professional forester to survey each tree individually. Your inventory will probably fall somewhere in the middle. Collect this minimum information about each tree:

- Species and Location such as address;
- Size in diameter;
- Site characteristics such as the amount of space between the curb and the sidewalk;
- Condition.

The scope of a tree inventory is determined by community goals. Examples of additional information that may be useful are:

- Tree maintenance needs
- Presence of overhead electrical lines
- Safety problems such as low hanging branches over streets or sidewalk
- Sidewalk damage.

CARE ABOUT TREES

Would you like your trees to live long, healthy lives? Maintenance is the key. Trees need a little extra care when they grow out of their natural habitat. In some situations, it is amazing that trees survive the daily onslaughts to their health and longevity. There are things we can do to prevent or lessen the effects of these factors on tree growth. Give trees regular care throughout their lives.

Water

Your established tree needs the equivalent of at least one inch of rainfall per week. If there are drought conditions, they need additional watering. Before you water a tree, check to see how dry the soil is by putting your finger into the soil under the mulch. To make fast work of checking soil moisture, invest in a soil moisture meter. Inexpensive meters are available at garden supply stores. Choose one with a probe long enough to reach through the mulch and a few inches into the soil.

If the soil is dry, add water. To water with a hose, lay it on the ground and turn it on low. Let the water run awhile and then move it to another spot under the canopy of the tree, but away from the trunk. A half-hour to one hour is usually enough for a medium sized tree.

Don't over-water. If your soil is clay or is compacted, you need less frequent watering—don't drown your tree! Sprinkler systems installed to water grass can harm trees. The installation process cuts roots and causes tree decline. The frequent watering needed to keep grass green during the summer can keep tree roots soggy and unhappy and may kill the tree. If you have a sprinkler system, plant water-loving trees and aim the sprinkler heads away from the trunk of each tree.

Inspect

Look at your trees closely once in a while to catch problems at the early stages. The earlier you catch them, the easier they are to control. When you check trees for problems, look for:

- ***Symptoms of insect, disease or other injury:*** holes, spots, discolored or missing bark, change in leaf shape, change in leaf color, reduced number of leaves, branch dieback, cracks or splits in trunk or branches.
- ***Signs of insects or diseases:*** bugs, egg masses, webbing, fungal fruiting bodies such as spores and conks, oozing sap, holes or wounds in trunk or branches.
- ***Environmental "stressors"*** that will have an adverse impact on plant growth: changes in drainage patterns, construction, overhead or underground utility work, lawnmower wounds, weed whip wounds, lawn chemicals, rodents, too exposed, not enough space, vehicle and pedestrian traffic over root system.

Control Problems

Once you identify something that is causing problems for your plants, look for a solution by reading publications or by consulting a plant professional. Publications are available through the extension service, from local tree inspectors and on the internet. Control the problem by using appropriate cultural, mechanical or chemical control measures or by removing the source of the damage.

Control Weeds

Use mulch to control most weeds around established trees. Pull by hand any weeds that show up. As you pull, don't let soil get mixed into the mulch or your weed problem will multiply. If you spray weed-killer (herbicide) onto weeds that grow in the mulch around a tree, do it on a calm day and use great care to spray only the weed, not the tree. If you use weed-killer to maintain your lawn, stay away from trees and shrubs. A broadleaf weed-killer doesn't know the difference between a maple treeanda dandelion.

Mulch

Mulching is good for established trees for the same reasons that it is beneficial for new trees. Mulching areas under large trees can also solve the problem of poor grass growth where turf must compete for sunlight, nutrients and water. Use a mulch of shredded bark or woodchips that is about four inches thick. Keep the mulch about six inches away from the base of each tree or shrub. To prevent root damage, use an herbicide such as Round-up to kill turfgrass under an established tree. See the sidebar for herbicide alternatives. Do not use a rototiller near established trees–they harm roots. We do not recommend the use of landscape edging near trees unless it is the type that sits on the soil surface.

Wrap

To protect the south side of thin-barked trees, such as lindens, maples and crabapples, from winter sunscald, use a light-colored guard such as paper tree wrap. Protect the trunk from the ground to the first branch. Wrap in the fall and unwrap each spring until the tree develops rough bark.

Remove Stakes and Ties

One growing season is the limit for stakes and ties. If they have been on your tree for longer than that, take them off. Stakes and ties can harm a tree directly by damaging its bark. They can harm a tree indirectly by affecting the growth of the tree trunk. Blowing around in the wind cues trees to stiffen up and grow thicker in the trunk.

Fertilize

Hold on! Now that we have your attention, what we really want to say is that your tree probably does not need fertilizer. Established trees only need fertilizer if they show symptoms of a nutrient deficiency. Rule out other problems first. We urge caution because when over applied, fertilizer can cause more harm than good. Fertilize young, vigorous trees, but hold back if your trees are past adolescence.

Prune

For established trees, prune to remove dead and damaged branches, and to eliminate hazards such as low-hanging branches. Remove branches that obstruct a desirable view or that rub on another branch, building or structure. If branches are near electric utility lines, call your electric utility to prune them. Train your young tree to have a single central leader (trunk) with well spaced, strong side branches. Plan to do most pruning during the winter when trees are dormant. Established trees which show no deficiency symptoms do not need to be fertilized. Young trees may benefit from the application of fertilizer the second autumn after planting and occasionally after that. Tree experts recommend fertilization to treat some specific tree problems such as nutrient deficiency.

Plant Nutrients

The major elements in fertilizers used for landscape plants are nitrogen (N), phosphorus (P) and potassium (K). Nitrogen is one of the most important elements for plant growth and is the most commonly deficient element because it moves around easily in the soil. A deficiency of nitrogen leads to yellowing of the leaves and reduced tree growth. A deficiency of phosphorus causes purple leaf coloration, small leaf size and early leaf drop. A deficiency of potassium leads to yellowing and death of leaf edges and tips, and branch dieback. Although most fertilizer formulations include phosphorus and potassium, most soils in Minnesota contain both in adequate quantities for plant growth. Sandy soils, which may be deficient in potassium, are an exception.

Iron and manganese are micronutrients that are important for plant growth and may be unavailable to plant roots in alkaline soils (pH above 7.0). The deficiency of these micronutrients leads to chlorosis or yellowing of leaves. Tree species which are susceptible to iron chlorosis include river birch, silver and red maple, and pin oak (particularly Eastern pin oak). Soil compaction and root injury may cause plants to exhibit symptoms of iron or manganese deficiency regardless of soil pH. Avoid chlorosis problems by planting species that tolerate alkaline soil if a soil test reveals alkaline conditions.

We recommend that you test soil before fertilizing a tree or shrub. Soil tests provide useful information about soil pH and major nutrients. In addition, look for plant symptoms as an indicator of whether or not a tree needs to be fertilized. Short annual twig growth, many dead branches, thin leaf canopy, reduced leaf size, light green or yellowgreen leaf color, and early fall coloration or defoliation may indicate a nutrient deficiency.

When to Fertilize

When we do fertilize, we prefer to do it in the fall after the leaves drop off. Early spring, before leaves emerge, is our second choice. Avoid fertilizing trees during the summer unless they are under regular irrigation. Fertilizing at this time of year may encourage new growth which may not have time to harden off adequately before cold weather sets in. It may also encourage some diseases, such as fireblight.

How to Fertilize

Complete fertilizers containing nitrogen, phosphorus and potassium come in organic and inorganic forms. Organic fertilizers such as manure and compost release nutrients slowly as they decompose. This reduces root burn and helps condition the soil. They usually contain a low amount of nitrogen and are more expensive than synthetic fertilizers.

The numbers in the fertilizer formulation refer to the percentages of each different nutrient (N-P-K) in the fertilizer. A fertilizer with a formulation of 18-8-5 contains 18 percent nitrogen, 8 percent phosphorus and 5 percent potassium by weight.

Nitrogen, used alone, may be broadcast over the soil underneath the crown of the tree and beyond at a rate of two to four pounds per 1,000 square feet. If there is turfgrass under the tree, do not use more than two pounds of actual nitrogen per 1,000 square feet of area or the grass will be harmed.

When there is grass competition, it is best to put the fertilizer directly into the soil below the turf by means of a root feeder, or by drilling holes and filling them with granular fertilizer, according to label directions. We do not recommend use of fertilizer spikes. Most absorbing roots of trees are within the top 12 inches of soil and are concentrated away from the trunk. Roots extend past the branch spread or "dripline" of the tree.

After you finish fertilizing, you may fill the openings to the top with sand, soil, vermiculite or peat moss to avoid fertilizer burn on the turfgrass. Holes made in the soil in the process of fertilizing have the added benefits of lessening soil compaction and increasing the amount of water and air which reach the roots. After you apply dry granular fertilizer by either broadcast or soil incorporation methods, water the tree well.

We recommend fertilizers which have a slow or controlled release of nitrogen. The nitrogen is supplied to the roots over a period of weeks or months. Slow-release fertilizer is especially helpful in areas where nitrogen leaches quickly through the soil, such as in sandy soils.

Example Calculation

- You want to fertilize a mature shade tree at the rate of 2 pounds of actual nitrogen (N) per 1,000 square feet of soil area.

- You drilled holes under the tree's branch spread and beyond. The area measures 35 feet by 35 feet (1,225 square feet).
- You have a 40 pound bag of fertilizer with a formulation of 15-5-5 (N-P-K). Since 15 percent of the weight of the bag is nitrogen, it contains 6 pounds (.15 x 40 pounds) of actual nitrogen. At a rate of 2 pounds of nitrogen per 1,000 square feet of area, this bag contains enough fertilizer for 3,000 square feet of area.
- Since you want to apply nitrogen at the rate of 2 pounds. per 1,000 square feet of area, you need a little less than 2½ pounds of nitrogen to cover the area under your tree.
- You decide to use about 17 pounds (2½/6 x 40) of this fertilizer and divide it equally among the holes you drilled.

PRUNE TREES

The pruning you do when your tree is young affects it throughout its life. Tree branches do not move and they usually do not change direction, so little problems grow into big problems. Trees in unnatural places, like on a boulevard, do not grow the same as their cousins in the natural forest. Trees in the natural forest grow close together. Lower branches do not get a lot of sun. They stay small and eventually die. The strongest trees make it to maturity. Life in town is different. It is up to people to prune trees so they grow up strong and healthy.

Has it been a long time since your tree was pruned? Take a look at your trees. A young tree needs pruning every year or two. Older trees need pruning at least once every five years. Too often, tree owners delay pruning until a tree looks unsightly. Then they prune for appearance. The result may be a tree that looks okay, but is full of defects that set the stage for storm damage and premature death. Even worse is the old technique of topping trees, which leads to trees full of defects and decay. Prune your tree for safety and tree health first. Consider appearance after that.

Pruning Priorities

For Safety

- Remove dead, damaged or broken branches.
- Remove weakly attached branches.
- Train your young tree to have one main trunk by pruning off branches, called double leaders, that turn up and compete with it. Train it to have well-spaced, well-attached side branches.
- Remove branches that interfere with the sidewalk, the street or other human needs.
- Remove branches that grow toward electrical power lines. Keep in mind that trees are good electrical conductors. If branches are near electrical lines already, contact your electrical utility. Let professionals, with their special equipment handle branches that are near lines.

For Health

- If two branches cross or rub, remove the least desirable branch.
- Remove diseased and low vigor branches, suckers and watersprouts.
- Prune low, temporary branches, so they stay small. That way they won't leave a big wound when they are finally cut off.
- If a branch rubs on a sign, a wire, a building or anything else that might damage the bark, remove it or prune it back to a side branch that is growing in a different direction.
- Thin branches for good structure, air movement, light penetration and/or weight reduction.
- Look for girdling roots. You may want to cut them before they strangle the tree.

For Appearance

Before you prune for appearance, consider these questions:

- What is the natural shape and character of this tree?

- What is the function of this tree? If a tree is supposed to slow the winter winds or block an unsightly view, do not remove the lower branches that do that job. If a tree is supposed to frame a view, not hide it, remove any branches that are in the way (A word of caution here: Be patient and let your young tree get tall enough before you remove lower branches). You can remove selected branches from the crown of the tree to allow a view of something as long as you do not remove more than onefourth of the foliage of the tree.

You can tell the difference between a strong branch attachment and one that is weak. Learn to recognize branch collars and never damage one with a pruning cut. Plan which branches to remove so that over the years your tree develops well spaced side branches. For a strong tree, the side branches should be less than one half as wide as the main trunk.

Before you prune, inspect your tree from the top down and plan the work. Remember tree safety and health come before appearance. Make pruning cuts with respect for the trees natural defense system. Make cuts at branch unions. Leave branch collars. Use sharp tools and make smooth cuts. There should not be any loose bark around the cut. Use three cuts to remove any branch that is too big to hold in your hand.

When you must cut a branch back to a side branch, it should be large enough to become the new leader. Select a side branch that is at least one third as wide as the branch that you will cut off.

There is usually no need to cover tree wounds with wound dressing. Trees do just fine all by themselves. If you must cover a wound (as in oak trees wounded April 15 to July 1) use a thin coating of latex paint. In the spring, sap will flow from pruning wounds on a maple or a birch. It is not harmful to the tree.

Try to leave trees alone when leaves are forming or falling. During these times, the tree is busy doing other things. It does not have energy to deal with pruning wounds. Winter, while trees are dormant, is a great time to prune trees. Removing dead branches is always beneficial to a tree regardless of the time of year.

Pruning Prescription for a Young Tree

- Prune every one to two years.
- Most pruning will involve removing live branches. Limit pruning to one fourth of the live branches per year.
- Look specially for branches that turn up and compete with the leader (trunk) of the tree. Remove the competing branches or head them back to slow down their growth.
- Leave lower branches on the tree for several years. Since tree branches stay in the same place all their life, you must remove the low, temporary branches as the tree gets taller. Keep them small relative to the trunk until it's time for removal.
- Select the main side (scaffold) branches. They should be well spaced along the trunk: about 1½ feet apart on large maturing trees. For small maturing trees, such as crabapples, 6-8 inches is adequate.
- Remove broken, split or rubbing branches, and those that interfere with the tree trunk or the main branches.

Pruning Prescription for a Middle Aged Tree

- Prune every two to four years
- If you need a ladder or a chainsaw, hire a professional arborist
- Remove fewer live branches than you would on a young tree
- Continue to prune as for a young tree to develop a strong trunk and well spaced, well attached branches
- Remove problem branches
- As the height of the tree increases, remove lower branches in the bottom one third of the tree. This is important where low branches may grow to interfere with streets, sidewalks, signs, buildings or other human needs. Consider the natural form of the tree and the job it is supposed to do in the landscape.

Pruning Prescription for a Mature Tree

- Hire a professional arborist to prune the tree every five years
- Get the dead out. Expect to remove a lot of dead branches and only a few live ones. Never remove more than one fourth of the live foliage in a single season
- Some old, dead branches have collars that are grown out along the branch. Remove only the dead branch, leaving the live collar uninjured.

Pollarding and espalier pruning are specialty training systems that are beyond the scope of this manual. Both are acceptable methods of training trees, so long as they are implemented properly and the tree owner is willing to do the annual or bi-annual maintenance that they require forever. Pollarding is not the same as topping.

Pruning Prescription for a Storm Damaged Tree

- A seriously damaged tree may need replacement
- Hire a professional arborist to prune the tree if there are broken or cracked branches higher than you can reach from the ground or if you need a chainsaw
- Properly prune dead, dying, broken or cracked branches
- If you must leave a branch whose end is broken, remove only the broken part without cutting into the undamaged part.
- Remove loose bark, but use care not to disturb live bark that is still attached to wood.
- Wait one growing season to prune for appearance
- Never top a storm damaged tree!

Work With Existing Trees

Is This Tree Worth Saving?

Trees age right along with humans. While healthy trees are desirable and add value to commercial and residential property, declining and dead trees decrease property values and may be a liability. Before deciding whether or not to remove a large, living tree, consider these key points:

What kind of tree is it?

Some types have a long life, attractive form, strong wood and other characteristics which make them a desirable part of the landscape.

Is the Tree Structurally Sound?

Some types of trees are brittle, have poor branch unions or other structural defects, such as decay or cracks, which make them potentially more hazardous. Not all trees with a defect fail and not all trees that fail are defective. Storm and construction damage may cause previously sound trees to become hazardous

Where is the Tree located?

If the tree is interfering with utilities, roads, walkways or buildings, or if it is in the way of a construction project, it may need to be removed. A tree with a defect may be hazardous if located near a target (house, play area, patio, parking area or street) upon which it could fall and damage a structure or injure people.

Does the Tree have Historic or Sentimental Value?

If the tree or the site was involved in an historic event that is of significance to local citizens, efforts should be made to retain the tree. If the tree was planted as a memorial, it may be undesirable or difficult to remove it.

Protect Trees from Construction Damage

Construction damage is one of the biggest killers of mature trees. Grade change involving soil fill or removal, soil compaction, root cutting, trunk wounds and changes in soil drainage patterns all harm existing trees. Some trees must be sacrificed when building on a wooded site; however, much of the tree injury which occurs could be avoided by following some simple guidelines:

- Go over the site with a professional arborist or forester before any equipment appears on the site.

- Determine which trees should be retained and mark them clearly.
- Meet the building contractor on site to discuss building and utility placement and agree upon which trees are to be protected.
- Protect designated trees with a sturdy barrier of snow fencing; to protect the root system, this barrier should be placed at a minimum distance from the trunk of one foot per inch of trunk diameter.
- Instruct all workers on the site regarding the reason for the barriers and that the barriers are not to be violated or removed.
- Pile soil and building materials away from protected trees.
- Place parking and driving areas away from protected trees.
- Avoid putting more than 3-4 inches of fill dirt over the root system of a tree in any one year. If fill must be applied, use a porous soil rather than clay subsoil. Temporary fill dirt should be removed within two months of application or the tree will be harmed. If more than four inches of fill must be added or removed in order to landscape the lot, consider a retaining wall or the addition of a drainage/aeration system around the tree's root system.
- Before excavating close to mature trees cut roots cleanly with a vibratory plow to reduce root tearing.
- Have underground utilities put in a common trench, if possible.
- Tunnel directly under the trunks of large trees instead of cutting major roots to put in utility lines.
- Place footings for decks and holes for fence supports where they will do the least harm to tree roots.
- Healthy, young trees will withstand construction injury better than mature, established trees. Oaks are particularly sensitive to construction damage. Take extra care when building or remodeling on a site containing these valuable trees.

- To improve the health of trees affected by construction damage, prune dead and dying limbs, aerate compacted soil, water trees well (unless drainage is poor) and mulch the root system with 4 inches of wood chips.
- Prior to construction, fertilize trees with a complete, slow-release, fertilizer. Use a fertilizer which has the same or less nitrogen than phosphorus and potassium. If trees are severely damaged, do not fertilize until the trees show signs of recovery.
- Water! Drought stressed trees are the trees most likely to die during or after construction activities.

Is this Tree Hazardous?

Inspect trees annually for hazardous conditions. Keep in mind that large, older trees and trees damaged by storms are often more dangerous than young, sound, uninjured trees. Fast-growing tree species and those which tend to form double-trunks and V-shaped crotches with included bark should also be examined more often for problems. Trees which have suffered construction damage, have root or trunk wounds, or are growing on severely compacted soil should also be examined, particularly if the crown of the tree is off-color or thin. Look for these warning signs of a hazardous tree:

- Dead tree.
- Cavities or decay in the trunk, branches or at the soil line, woodpecker holes or shelf fungi.
- Cracks in a large branch; cracks where the branches meet the trunk; cracks in the main trunk, particularly if they occur on opposite sides or extend into the ground.
- Dead branches in the crown that are more than 1 inch in diameter.
- Leaning trees, particularly if the lean is recent and there are signs of soil disturbance or exposed roots.
- Trunk wounds or cankers.
- Branch drop of seemingly healthy large branches may indicate internal decay.

When looking for hazards, consider the history of the tree. Was it was ever topped or wounded? Trees tend to grow wood over their wounds, so internal defects are not always obvious. If you doubt the soundness of a tree, consult a tree professional. If there is no target present (see sidebar) dead or decayed trees, or tree trunks, can be preserved for wildlife habitat.

Scientists learn about climate and how it has changed by studying climates of the past. By analyzing changes that have occurred in the earth's temperature over time, scientists can gain a better understanding of global warming, and make determinations about its possible causes.

Scientists have discovered ways to study the earth's climate, going back as far as thousands, or even millions, of years. Those who specialize in studying ancient climates are known as paleoclimatologists, a name derived from the Greek root word *paleo*, which means ancient. Paleoclimatologists use natural elements in the environment to find "proxy climate data" related to the past. When they study these types of data, these scientists typically use several different methods, so they are assured of forming the most accurate analysis possible.

Tree Rings Tell a Story

One way that paleoclimatologists unlock the secrets of ancient climates is by studying the rings in certain types of trees, such as the redwoods and giant sequoias found in California and different varieties of pines. As a tree grows, it adds a new layer of wood to its trunk every year. This forms a ring, and the age of the tree can be determined by counting the number of these annual growth rings.

Many trees live to be hundreds of years old, and some live for thousands of years. The oldest trees on Earth are the bristlecone pines, many of which are found in the Ancient Bristlecone Pine Forest in California's White Mountains. The average age of these trees is 1,000 years, and a few are more than 4,000 years old. In 1964, before there were environmental laws to protect ancient trees, a particular bristlecone pine named Prometheus was cut down. After analyzing the tree's rings, scientists determined that the tree had been 4,862 years old—the oldest living thing on Earth.

Paleoclimatologists can learn more than just the age of a tree by studying its rings. They can determine what sort of climate conditions existed during its life by analyzing the thickness of each tree ring. Thick rings are a sign of favorable climate, abundant rainfall, and good growing conditions. Thin rings indicate poor growing conditions and lack of rain, as well as natural disasters such as droughts, floods, and volcanoes.

Samples from trees can be obtained in several different ways. Scientists do not want to needlessly destroy living trees, so they cut cross sections only from dead trees, logs, or stumps. These can be found intact on the ground, buried deep in the ground, or submerged in water. Tree remnants that have been buried for hundreds or even thousands of years have been found and analyzed. For samples from living trees, scientists use a tool known as an increment borer to drill a thin hole into the trunk. Then, a core sample of wood about the size of a drinking straw is extracted for analysis. This boring does not cause damage to the tree because when the sample has been removed, the tree naturally closes the small opening just as it would close a wound caused by insects or weather. Tree rings like these not only tell scientists the age of the tree, but they also provide a record of climate change over the centuries.

Once the wood samples are obtained, scientists return to the laboratory to measure and date them. Cross sections of dead trees are often old and brittle; and scientists may need to glue pieces together—or mount them on a hard wooden surface—for added protection. Cores that are taken from living trees are soft, so they must be dried before being mounted for examination. The next step is to sand the samples or trim them with razor blades to produce a smooth surface that makes the fine details of the rings more visible. Then scientists can examine the samples under a microscope and record their findings about the tree's history.

Clues Beneath the Water

Another way paleoclimatologists analyze historical climates is by studying samples of varves—layers of silt and clay that are deposited year after year on the bottoms of glacial lakes and ponds. Varves provide natural climate records going back several thousand years. They consist of two layers: a thick, light-colored layer of silt and fine sand that forms in the spring and summer, and a thinner, dark-colored layer of clay that forms in the fall and winter and sinks to the bottom.

Varve thickness varies from year to year, usually according to the climate and the amount of rain that falls during a particular season. For example, when temperatures are especially hot and dry and there is little rain, less soil is washed into the water, and the varve layers are thinner. On the other hand, when spring and summer rains are heavy, a greater amount of soil is washed into lakes and ponds, and this causes thicker varves. Paleoclimatologists collect varve samples by using long, hollow tubes to drill into the soft bottoms of lakes and ponds. Once they extract this material, they analyze the different layers that have been deposited over time.

Clues about ancient climates are not found only in bodies of freshwater such as lakes and ponds, but are also buried in sediment that has settled in the earth's deep oceans. Robert B. Gagosian says that by studying these sediments, called deep-sea cores, scientists can reconstruct the history of ocean climates spanning thousands of years. He describes this research, and explains why it is so important:

> Preserved in the sediments are the fossil remains of microscopic organisms that settle to the seafloor. They accumulate over time in layers . . . that delineate many important aspects of past climate. For instance, certain organisms are found only in colder, polar waters and never live in warmer waters. They can reveal where and when cold surface waters existed—and didn't exist—in the past. From records like these, we know that about 12,800 years ago, North Atlantic waters cooled dramatically—and so did the North Atlantic region. This large cooling in Earth's climate . . . lasted for about 1,300 years. This period is called the Younger Dryas, and it is just one of several periods when Earth's climate changed very rapidly from warm to cold conditions, and then back to warm again.

To gather data from oceans, scientists spend two to three months on research cruises. Using highly specialized equipment, they remove samples of deep-sea cores from beneath the surface of the ocean floor. These long cylinders of sediment provide valuable evidence about changes in ocean temperatures that were caused by fluctuations in climate.

Scientists also gather and study sediment from different bodies of water to gather pollen. This powdery substance, produced by flowering plants each growing season, is carried in the wind, and billions of grains of it end up buried at the bottoms of lakes, ponds, rivers, and oceans. The oldest pollen becomes fossilized, and is often found in sedimentary rocks that have formed over thousands of years. Since all plant species produce their own unique type of pollen, scientists can *Marine fossils such as these provide clues about climatic conditions during the fossilized creatures' lifetime.* tell what plants grew during certain periods in the earth's history. Also, they can make accurate estimates about changes in climate. This is because for every type of pollen, certain habitat conditions would have been necessary for that particular kind of plant to survive and thrive.

Underwater Cities

Coral reefs can also provide important clues to climates of the past. There are many different types of corals, but "stony corals" build huge reefs in warm, tropical seas. Coral reefs are made up of millions of tiny animals called coral polyps, which are cousins of the jellyfish. Although polyps differ in size, they are usually quite small—about the size of a pinhead. The polyps form protective skeletons by extracting calcium carbonate—the same material that is found in teeth, bones, and shells—from the salty, tropical ocean waters in which they live. As the skeletons grow, coral reefs are formed, and become as hard as rocks. These huge structures are often called underwater.

Coral reefs have grown to gigantic proportions over the centuries. Scientists study a reef's layers to learn about long-term climate changes. cities because they are the largest biologically built structures on Earth.

Every time a piece of coral skeleton is created, it leaves a record of the conditions under which it was created. For instance, when water temperatures change, the chemistry (or makeup) of the skeletons also changes. The result is that coral formed in the summer looks different than coral formed in the winter, so it is easy for paleoclimatologists to know in which season the coral was formed. As coral reefs grow, growth bands form that are very much like the growth rings found in trees. Sometimes these bands are visible to the naked eye, and sometimes scientists can only see the bands by x-raying them.

To gather samples of coral, scientists go on diving expeditions in tropical areas, where they search for massive coral reefs built by stony coral. Using drills that are connected to a compressor mechanism on a ship, the divers extract cores of the coral, much the same way cores are extracted from trees. Their goal is to drill in areas where the most growth has occurred, as the NOAA explains: "Think of the coral's structure as being very similar to an onion sliced in half, with a new ring added each year. If you wanted to drill into an onion to sample as many rings as possible, you would core from the surface directly towards the center. This is exactly how scientists go about getting as long a sample as possible from each coral."

Once scientists have carefully extracted the cores, they label and box them for shipment to their laboratories. There they x-ray the coral to examine the growth bands, which helps them determine the seasons in which the corals grew. With this proxy climate data, paleoclimatologists can analyze how climates fluctuated in the reef over hundreds of years.

Unlocking Secrets in Ancient Ice

Just as scientists gain clues about climate from warm, tropical seas, they can also gather knowledge from the coldest places on the earth. In fact, some of the most revealing indicators of historical climates come from studies of glaciers and ice sheets in the world's polar regions. To gather samples of ancient ice, scientists travel to remote areas of Antarctica, where temperatures can dip as low as -129 degrees Fahrenheit.

Massive ice domes, ice sheets, and glaciers are found in the Arctic and in Antarctica. These ice formations developed over hundreds of thousands of years as layers of snow pressed together. More precipitation continued to pile on top of the snow, squeezing the layers and slowly forming ice. As the layers accumulated, air bubbles were trapped inside, forming distinct lines that can be counted as easily as tree rings. Scientists examine the layers to determine the age of the ice and the approximate climate during a given period. They can also tell how much snow fell during a year, as well as what kind of air, dust, volcanic material, and other microscopic particles—including pollution—existed at the time the ice sheets were formed.

About 98 per cent of the world's ancient ice is located in the polar regions, and most scientists choose to focus on those areas when they study ice. Others, however, believe that ice from tropical areas is even more crucial in order to understand how climates have changed over time. Lonnie Thompson is a glaciologist who studies ancient ice in areas such as South America and Africa. These regions have hot, tropical climates, but they also have very high mountain ranges where ice sheets and glaciers can be found. Thompson sometimes climbs mountains three or four miles high. On one expedition, he and his team worked for three weeks at an altitude above twenty-three thousand feet.

Thompson's work is challenging as weli as dangerous. With the help of local porters and animals called yaks, he and his team haul about six tons.

This mammoth Antarctic glacier dwarfs the scientist at its base. Glacial ice cores give scientists a historical record of climate changes.

equipment to the top of a mountain. There they must endure bone-chilling cold, the threat of avalanches, and such high altitudes that it is hard to breathe. There is also the risk of frequent windstorms. One particularly fierce storm knocked Thompson's tent from its moorings and nearly blew him off a mountain.

During a typical expedition, Thompson and his team accumulate about four tons of ice samples, which means they must drag ten tons of equipment back down the mountain. He says it is well worth the effort, though, and he explains why he thinks ice is the best possible archive of the history of the earth's climate: "Understanding how the climate system works and has worked in the natural system is absolutely essential for any prediction of what's going to happen to the climate in the future." Thompson adds that by examining ancient ice, scientists can determine climate conditions and changes over thousands of years in the past.

Whether they explore ice domes in Antarctica, glaciers in Tibet, or ice sheets at the top of Africa's Kilimanjaro, scientists gather samples by using powerful drills to bore into the ice. The deeper the drill goes—and that can be several miles—the further it travels back in time. (Thompson's oldest ice sample is more than seven hundred thousand years old.) After drilling, scientists extract cores of ice and carefully package them in insulated containers, so the samples can be sent to their laboratories for analysis. Thompson says that by collecting ice samples, scientists can compile a frozen history of the earth.

Modern Instruments for Measuring

The reason scientists use proxy climate data obtained from ice, trees, coral reefs, and other products of nature is because they want to understand what the earth's climate was like long ago. Scientists use these types of data along with modern devices so they can learn more about how climate has changed over time, as well as how historical and current climates compare with each other.

Thermometers, which measure temperatures of the earth's surface, have been used to determine climate for only about 130 years. Some scientists, like Dr. S. Fred Singer, who is an atmospheric physicist, question the accuracy of thermometers because they are often used near cities, which are warmer than open country. Singer explains his views: "You have to be very careful with surface record. . . . As cities expand, they get warmer. And therefore they affect the readings. And it's very difficult to eliminate this—what's called the urban heat island effect."

One can find empty holes in the ground—abandoned oil wells, for instance—and put down a long line of thermometers.

This allows measurement of the temperature of soil or rocks many levels down. The reason this works is because over time, the warmth at the surface is conducted to deeper levels. So, the temperature deep down in the hole relates to the surface temperature of long ago. This is also true when the surface is cold—the coolness is conducted down over time. Many holes have been measured in recent years, and what we've found is that the record of past temperatures confirms what is measured from carefully placed surface thermometers.

Watching from Space

A highly sophisticated way of monitoring the earth's climate is through the use of satellites. Since the 1950s, NASA satellites have been observing Earth's atmosphere, oceans, land, snow, and ice from high in space. The data they provide can help scientists develop a better understanding of how these different elements interact with each other to influence climate and weather.

One example is *Terra*, a satellite that was launched by NASA in 1999. *Terra*, named after the Latin word for land, is about the size of a small school bus, and its mission is to circle Earth for about six years. The satellite is fitted with a variety of sensitive instruments that are designed for specific purposes, such as measuring the chemical composition of clouds and gauging the temperature of the land. *Terra*'s MICR instrument has nine separate digital cameras that take pictures of Earth from different angles, while its MOPITT instrument uses light sensors to measure concentrations of methane gas and carbon monoxide, two heat-trapping gases. The satellite's instrument MODIS measures cloud cover and also monitors changes in Earth due to fires, earthquakes, droughts, or flooding. An instrument called CERES measures both incoming energy from the sun and reflected energy from Earth and studies the role that clouds play in this energy balance.

In the spring of 2002, NASA launched another satellite called *Aqua*, whose mission is to gather information about the earth's bodies of water. *Aqua* will circle the planet every sixteen days for six years, and its sophisticated instruments will measure such things as global precipitation, evaporation, humidity, and ocean circulation. This data will help scientists better understand the balance between the earth's oceans, land, and atmosphere, as well as how *the* Aqua *satellite gathers data about a hurricane visible on Earth's surface.* Aqua's *data helps scientists understand global climatic changes.* global climate change influences this balance.

In the future, NASA will launch more satellites to study global climate change. The organization describes the goal for these studies as follows:

> As we learn more about our home planet, new questions arise, drawing us deeper into the complexities of Earth's climate system. We don't know the answers to many other important questions, like: Is the current warming trend temporary, or just the beginning of an accelerating increase in global temperatures? As temperatures rise, how will this affect weather patterns, food production systems, and sea level? Are the number and size of clouds increasing and, if so, how will this affect the amount of incoming and reflected sunlight, as well as the heat emitted from Earth's surface? . . . How will climate change affect human health, natural resources, and human economies in the future? NASA's Earth Observing System, and Terra in particular, will help scientists answer these questions, as well as some we don't even know to ask yet.

Unraveling the Mystery

Scientists are the first to say that there are many unknown factors involved in the study of global climate change. Products of nature such as ice cores, coral reefs, ocean and lake sediments, and trees can offer valuable clues about changing climates in the ancient past. Modern instruments like satellites can provide knowledge about current activities affecting the earth's land, oceans, and atmosphere. Assembling the pieces of this global environmental puzzle is the focus of scientists and researchers all over the world. They know for sure that the earth is warming—and using the many tools available to them, it is their mission to find out why.

4

TREE RING DATING

INTRODUCTION

Ring dating (dendrochronology) has been used in an attempt to extend the calibration of carbon-14 dating earlier than historical records allow. The oldest *living* trees, such as the Bristlecone Pines (*Pinus longaeva*) of the White Mountains of Eastern California, were dated in 1957 by counting tree rings at 4,723 years old. This would mean they pre-dated the Flood which occurred around 4,350 years ago, taking a straight-forward approach to Biblical chronology.

However, when the interpretation of scientific data contradicts the true history of the world as revealed in the Bible, then it's the interpretation of the data that is at fault. It's important to remember that we have limited data, and new discoveries have often overturned previous 'hard facts'.

Recent research on seasonal effects on tree rings in other trees in the same genus, the plantation pine *Pinus radiata*, has revealed that up to five rings per year can be produced and extra rings are often indistinguishable, even under the microscope, from annual rings. Evidence of false rings in *any* woody tree species would cast doubt on claims that any particular species has *never* in the past produced false rings. Evidence from *within the same genus* surely counts much more strongly against such a notion. Creationists have shown that the Biblical kind is usually larger than the 'species' and in many cases even larger than the 'genus'.

Considering that the immediate post-Flood world would have been wetter with less contrasting seasons until the Ice Age waned, many extra growth rings would have been produced in the Bristlecone pines (even though extra rings are not produced today because of the seasonal extremes). Taking this into account would bring the age of the oldest living Bristlecone Pine into the post-Flood era.

Claimed older tree ring chronologies depend on the cross-matching of tree ring patterns of pieces of dead wood found near living trees. This procedure depends on temporal placement of fragments of wood using carbon-14 (^{14}C) dating, assuming straight-line extrapolation backwards of the carbon dating. Having placed the fragment of wood approximately using the ^{14}C data, a matching tree-ring pattern is sought with wood that has a part with overlapping ^{14}C age and that also extends to a younger age. A tree ring pattern that matches is found close to where the carbon 'dates' are the same. And so the tree-ring sequence is extended from the living trees backwards.

Now superficially this sounds fairly reasonable. However, it is a circular process. It assumes that it is approximately correct to linearly extrapolate the carbon 'clock' backwards. There are good reasons for doubting this. The closer one gets back to the Flood the more inaccurate the linear extrapolation of the carbon clock would become, perhaps radically so. Conventional carbon-14 dating assumes that the system has been in equilibrium for tens or hundreds of thousands of years, and that ^{14}C is thoroughly mixed in the atmosphere. However, the Flood buried large quantities of organic matter containing the common carbon isotope, ^{12}C, so the $^{14}C/^{12}C$ ratio would rise after the Flood, because ^{14}C is produced from nitrogen, not carbon. These factors mean that early post-Flood wood would look older than it really is and the 'carbon clock' is not linear in this period.

The biggest problem with the process is that ring patterns are not unique. There are many points in a given sequence where a sequence from a new piece of wood match well (note that even two trees growing next to each other will not have *identical* growth ring patterns). Yamaguchi1 recognized that ring pattern matches are not unique. The best match (using statistical tests) is often rejected in favour of a less exact match because the best match is deemed to be 'incorrect' (particularly if it is too far away from the carbon-14 'age'). So the carbon 'date' is used to constrain just which match is acceptable. Consequently, the calibration is a circular process and the tree ring chronology extension is also a circular process that is dependent on assumptions about the carbon dating system.

The extended tree ring chronologies are far from absolute, in spite of the popular hype. To illustrate this we only have to consider the publication and subsequent withdrawal of two European tree-ring chronologies. According to David Rohl,3 the Sweet Track chronology from Southwest England was 're-measured' when it did not agree with the published dendrochronology from Northern Ireland (Belfast). Also, the construction of a detailed sequence from southern Germany was abandoned in deference to the Belfast chronology, even though the authors of the German study had been confidant of its accuracy until the Belfast one was published. It is clear that dendrochronology is not a clear-cut, objective dating method despite the extravagant claims of some of its advocates.

Extended tree ring chronology is not an independent confirmation/calibration of carbon dating earlier than historically validated dates, as has been claimed.

For a number of years trees in excess of 4000 years of age have been reported and, quite naturally, there has been widespread interest in anything that could live to such an age . This interest is further heightened by the beauty of the subject—the bristlecone pines and their surroundings. These trees grow in the White Mountains of east-central California and have been artistically twisted and sculptured by their harsh environment.

Several factors have been suggested as contributing to the longevity of the bristlecone pines: slow growth due to soil conditions and relative aridity; sparse ground cover incapable of supporting a destructive fire; highly resinous and dense wood resistant to decay and insects; and needles that are retained for 20 to 30 years, providing a photosynthetic capacity for spanning many years of stressful conditions . Whatever the reasons for their success in survival, there can be little doubt that these trees are the oldest living things. The study of their wood is pertinent to climatology as well as chronology.

TREE-RING STUDY

When it's dry, it's dry all over, according to an analysis of more than 400 years of annual streamflow in the Upper Colorado and Salt and Verde river basins. Tree-ring study findings show that ancient droughts are geographically widespread, and droughts affect water supplies over a broad region.

By using data from tree rings, University of Arizona researchers conclude that water supply for those western rivers fluctuated in synchrony during periods of severe drought. The study goes back almost 800 years in the Salt-Verde basin and covers waterways from the states of Arizona, Colorado, New Mexico, Utah and Wyoming.

Overall conclusion is that severe droughts and low-flow conditions in one basin are unlikely to be offset by abundant streamflow in the other basin.

"Prior to the findings from this study, the conventional wisdom was that runoff from the Colorado River would be available to make up for deficits on the Salt and Verde rivers during times of extreme drought," said Charlie Ester, SRP's manager of Water Resource Operations. "The bottom line is that the Upper Colorado Basin and the Salt and Verde basins work together as one entire region."

Tree-ring-based reconstructions of streamflow can peer back into time much further than the records available from streamflow gauges. Such reconstructions could provide important insights into the hydrologic variability of a river basin over time.

The findings represent just the first phase of a study partnered by SRP and The University of Arizona's Laboratory of Tree-Ring Research. UA scientists Katherine K. Hirschboeck, an associate professor of climatology, and David M. Meko, an associate research professor, conducted the tree-ring analysis

THE RING DATA

Climate models predict that northern high latitudes will see an amplification of global warming from the greenhouse effect. Boreal forest ecosystems are sensitive to climatic and environmental shifts and may provide evidence of this warming; changes in the frequency of disturbance regimes in Alaskan boreal forests may already be in evidence. One of the focuses of my research is to investigate high-resolution (annual to decadal-scale) changes over the past several hundred years, a time frame highly relevant to the human perspective. Surprisingly, few studies have focused on this time period in Alaska. Two promising sources of this type of information are sediment cores from lakes with fast sedimentation rates, and tree rings. Recent work on finely spaced samples from cores collected in lakes of the PALE (Paleoclimates from Arctic Lakes and Estuaries) study indicates significant recent changes in the climate of interior Alaska. Conditions may have been much harsher in the early 1800s to mid-1800s. Tree ring studies offer a way of reconstructing climate prior to recorded meteorological data, which go back about 90 years in interior Alaska. Prior tree ring studies in interior Alaska have not focused on multiparameter climate reconstructions with annual resolution. My work focuses on utilizing multiproxy information from tree rings to reconstruct past changes in temperature and precipitation for interior Alaska over the past several hundred years and to look at how the general health of the forest stands have changed over time. In order to do this, the ring data must first be calibrated with the recorded meteorological data, which is the part of this study reported here.

The three different parameters of the annual tree rings (width, density, and ð13C isotope concentration) measured in this study produce distinctly different climatic information. Ring width is the parameter most commonly studied. Large, thin-walled cells are laid down early in the growing season when conditions are favorable for growth. These are followed by smaller, thick-walled and denser cells late in the growing season which form due to the onset of cooler temperatures, lack of soil moisture, and shorter days. The production of latewood cells terminates abruptly, followed by larger cells the following growing season. This abrupt termination at the end of one year and the beginning of the next year marks a ring boundary. Ring width is measured between two successive ring boundaries. In previous Alaskan studies, ring width has correlated with annual temperature.

Cell density is measured across the length and width of the tree ring, and there is intra-annual as well as inter-annual variation. Maximum density is the parameter that is typically measured and is usually correlated with summer temperatures here in Alaska. Wood density may be affected by factors other than those which affect tree ring width and may be more sensitive to environmental changes.

Stable carbon isotope ratio ($\delta^{13}C$) is correlated with moisture availability. This occurs because stomates remain open for longer periods when moisture is available, allowing for greater exchange of CO_2 and selection of lighter carbon. Thus under moisture-limiting conditions or arid climates, reduced CO_2 availability results in less discrimination against the heavier isotope and higher $\delta^{13}C$ values.

The combination of width, density, and isotope analysis offers a powerful set of independent but mutually reinforcing tools for reconstructing climate because the effects of temperature and precipitation can be distinguished, and seasonal changes can be observed. A better understanding of how the boreal forests are affected by different climate parameters is necessary to predict response to future climatic changes.

The results from the calibration part of this study (1909-1981) show maximum latewood density is significantly cor- related with May and August temperature (0.557 and 0.691) and August precipitation (-0.464). Normalized May and August temperature is correlated with density (0.791, 0.912 with 5-year running mean). Wood $\delta^{13}C$ ratios are negatively correlated with growth year precipitation (-0.488, -0.656 smoothed) and positively correlated (0.610, 0.857 smoothed) with May-August temperature. A combined index of normalized May-August temperature and yearly precipitation correlated with $\delta^{13}C$ at 0.710 (0.844 smoothed). The results of this calibration indicate that there is significant climatically driven stress on the trees from this stand when summer temperatures are high and annual precipitation is low. This combination of circumstances has occurred more frequently since the mid-1970s than at any other time during the twentieth century.

BACKGROUND OF TREE-RING DATING

The techniques and theories of tree ring dating (dendrochronology) have their foundation in the work of A.E. Douglass in the early part of this century . Douglass and his successors, Glock, Shulman, et al., were interested in climatic variations over long periods of time and turned to the examination of the variation in width of annual growth rings as a clue to climatic conditions for those annual periods. They were interested in groups of wide rings as evidence of seasons of plenteous rainfall and favorable growth conditions; groups of narrow rings suggested dry, stressful climatic conditions. Of course, they identified the time of occurrence of these climatic variations by counting the number of successive tree rings, but tree ring dating as it has developed consists of substantially more than simply counting the number of rings in a tree. Before examining the current techniques of tree ring dating we should review the fundamental principles of tree growth and the formation of rings.

Tree growth is confined to a layer of cells beneath the bark and wrapping the woody part of the tree. As this layer of cells, the cambium, produces more cells the tree grows in diameter. A typical growth cycle begins in the spring with the cambium laying down large, well-developed cells. As growing conditions become less favorable in the summer—less moisture, etc.—the cells formed are smaller, more dense, and have a dark appearance. In the fall and winter, growth largely stops. The cycle of rapid growth (large, light cells) and slower growth (small, dark cells) gives rise to the appearance of successive "rings" for each growing season. Counting these rings in a cross section of wood then gives an indication of the number of seasons of growth.

Two phenomena sometimes complicate the straight-forward situation described above. The first of these is "multiple ring" years. If, after summer has set in and small cells are being produced, sudden rains stimulate additional growth of large cells, a second ring of small cells will be produced when the growing season actually ends. It is relatively easy for a trained examiner to detect such occurrences because of the peculiar composition of the first or "false" rings of the season. The second and more difficult complication is that of "missing" rings. In dry and climatically harsh years, no detectable growth may occur. In this case no ring is formed and the ring is missing for that season or year. Such missing rings are not usually discovered directly but they may be inferred from a variety of data, including the actual tree ring dating process which we will now discuss.

BASIC PRINCIPLES

This principle is commonly applied, even by schoolboys, to determine the age of a freshly cut tree. If the cut is clean enough, the rings are counted and the age of the tree is presumed to be equal to the number of rings. Despite the possibility of some missing rings or multiple rings the procedure is basically valid and generally accepted.

The second principle is also simple but was not verified by observation until 1904. At that time A.E. Douglass had been studying the annual variation in the thickness of tree rings as a clue to climatic patterns. It seemed logical to him that the pattern of variation in ring widths (thicknesses) seen in one specimen of wood should be the same as that seen in other specimens that grew at the same time under the same environmental conditions. He made the crucial observation while casually examining the stumps of a cut-over forest in northern Arizona. What he saw was "sets of compact patterns of ring variation duplicated from one tree stump to another with such clarity as to be easily recognized without a ring count".

Suppose that a certain tree began growing in 1866 and another in 1890. In 1916 the first tree is cut down and fashioned into a large beam used as a structural element in a building. The other tree continues to grow until the present day at which time it also is cut down. Ideally, this second tree would be found to contain 83 annual rings (in 1973). If it has a distinctive growth pattern in its first 26 rings (counting from the center of the tree), this same distinctive growth pattern will probably be found in the beam from the first tree which was used for building in 1916. This would allow precise placement of the age of the wood used in the building with respect to the present, i.e., at least 57 years before present.

But more. Since the first tree was growing 24 years before the long-lived survivor, its additional rings extend the chronology pattern to 107 years. By correlating distinctive patterns in successively older specimens the chronology can be extended back into time as far as the specimen data permits.

Once the distinctive ring patterns are identified for the master chronology, any specimen found to contain a significant portion of the pattern is precisely dated. Applications to archaeology and other fields are apparent and have been successful.

Three Practical Difficulties

The fundamental prerequisite for cross matching is a distinctive pattern of ring widths. Unfortunately, such patterns are not as common as dendrochronologists might wish. In order for wood to exhibit a distinctive pattern it must have grown through a period when distinctive climatic variations occurred, and it must have been sensitive to this variation. Climatic variation is common but many trees grow in environments relatively insensitive to such variation. For example, trees growing on even terrain or lowlands where ample water supplies are always available (semipermanent water tables, etc.) will ordinarily not reflect year to year variations of climate. In other words, because they do not feel a significant variation in year to year stress they produce rings of the same size year after year. Their wood specimens are described as complacent (as opposed to distinctive) and are not suitable for cross matching. Distinctive patterns are most commonly found in specimens from stressful environments.

Climatic cycles with long periods (greater than 15 years) superimpose trends of increasing ring widths and decreasing ring widths on yearly variation. Also there is a general trend of decreasing ring width with age of the tree. These and other similar factors can largely be filtered out by the use of standard statistical methods. Difficulties of this type are presumed to be of minor significance.

A third and serious difficulty relates to the completeness of the data. The most distinctive features of a pattern and the most useful for cross matching are the "minimum" rings. These are the occasional extremely thin rings formed during a very stressed season. Unfortunately these are the rings most easily missed in tabulating the data. The magnitude of this problem is more readily appreciated when it is recognized that specimens with 10 rings per millimeter are sometimes included in chronologies. Microscopes and semiautomated instrumentation partially relieve this problem, but despite these aids, missing rings are a real and probably permanent hazard in tree-ring dating. The location of a few missing rings in a large specimen may be inferred when attempting to cross match, but when as high as five percent of the rings are missing, cross matching is obviously questionable if not futile.

A Successful Application

The middle of the nineteenth century was a period of territorial and political dispute in the American Southwest. The end of the Mexican War in 1848 was confirmed by the treaty of Guadalupe Hidalgo, which treaty explicitly acknowledged "all native claims." Amongst these legitimate claims were those of the Navajo Indian Tribe. Nevertheless, a number of years later all Navajos were forcibly removed from their lands and impounded on a distant reservation by the United States Army. In 1868 a treaty was executed between the United States and the Navajo Indians allowing them to return to their native lands.

The Congress has authorized the Navajos to bring substantiated claims for their rightful territories lost at the time of establishment of reservations. Of focal concern are the lands actually occupied during the period 1848-1868; although earlier occupation would have some relevance also.

Two independent lines of evidence have been presented with regards to several sites of occupation. The first of these are cultural records which include oral reports of early recollections and some substantiating documentation. The second line of evidence is based on tree-ring dating. Absolute master chronologies based on long-lived trees in the regions of interest have served to specifically date the remains of hogans and other Navajo artifacts . Of special interest is the fact that the cultural records corroborate the tree ring dates in establishing Navajo occupation during the period in question.

BRISTLECONE PINE CHRONOLOGY

The history of the development of the Bristlecone Pine chronology goes back to 1954 and the discovery by Edmund Schulman of several of these trees in excess of 4000 years of age. The chronology has now been extended by C. W. Ferguson to at least 7485 years (before present) with hopes of pushing it to perhaps 10,000 years.

The number of specimens cross matching for any given period averages about four. No information has been published on how well the specimens cross-matched, nor is data provided allowing such a check. However, partial statistical analyses of the quality of the component specimens are available.

Bearing in mind the principles and difficulties inherent in tree-ring dating, it is worthwhile to examine several features of the Bristlecone Pine chronology.

Bristlecone Pine Data Quality

"In bristlecone pine, problems of cross dating are caused by so-called 'missing' rings associated with the extremely slow growth rate of this species on and sites. One specimen, for example, contains more than 1100 annual rings in 12.7 centimeters of radius . . . In some instances, five percent or more of the annual rings may be missing along a given radius that spans many centuries." In fact, up to 10 percent of the rings may be missing along a given radius (6). This creates a situation where it is difficult if not impossible to find significant cross matches. This is especially true because it is generally the very narrow diagnostic rings which are "missing." In other words, the very rings responsible for the distinctiveness of a pattern are the ones most likely to be missing.

It is not surprising, then, to find that nearly 50 percent of the bristlecone pine samples used as components in the 7104-year master chronology have mean sensitivities of less than .30 . Such low sensitivities are suggestive of complacent samples that would cross match about the same regardless of where they were placed in the chronology.

"Ball-park" Placement

A preliminary search for regions of cross-matching usually involves visual comparison of what are called "skeleton plots." These plots illustrate the most distinctive features of a pattern and are a useful tool in the hands of competent researchers. However, it is extremely difficult to use such a procedure when dealing with samples containing hundreds of rings in comparisons with a master chronology with thousands of rings. Therefore, in the case of the bristlecone pine chronology, the expedient of determining initial placement by a radiocarbon date has been employed. In the words of the researcher, "I often am unable to date specimens with one or two thousand rings against a 7500-year master chronology, even with the 'ball-park' placement provided by a radiocarbon date". Two observations are in order here:

1. The construction of the bristlecone pine chronology is at least partially dependent on radiocarbon dating.

2. Complacent samples could be fit into the chronology reasonably well based on their radiocarbon dates and with "missing" rings supplied as needed. (Evidence pertinent to this possibility is presented in the next section.) Some elaboration is needed on the first point since the author quoted above claims that the bristlecone pine chronology "constitutes the first independent time control of such length for radiocarbon analysis" (emphasis supplied). The incongruity of such a claim lies in the fact that radiocarbon dating influences the dating of bristlecone pine specimens and then these specimens are used to calibrate radio carbondating.

The bristlecone pine chronology has generally been accepted as verifying the validity of radiocarbon dating for greater than 7000 years . Unless the chronology can be shown to be free of radiocarbon dating influence, such attempted verification is improper and invalid.

Pine Alpha "Missing" Rings

Pine Alpha was the first tree found to be over 5000 years old. It is also the only one of the bristlecone pines for which ring indices have been published.

It is noteworthy that this specimen is one of the more sensitive components of the master chronology; having a mean sensitivity of. In the figure certain minimum ring years are circled. These rings have been ambiguously referred to as "missing" rings. Whether these rings have been "supplied" or "found" is not clear. If the latter is the case no further comment is necessary. If the former is the case it should be noted that removal of these rings would yield a complacent sample not suitable for cross matching.

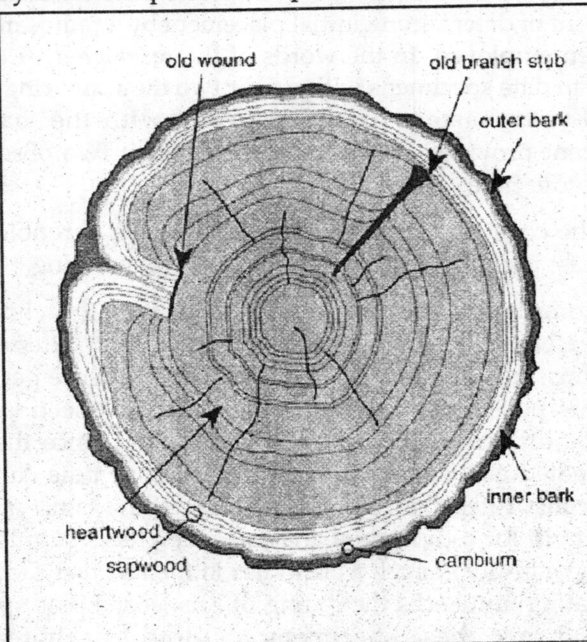

Fig. 4.1: A segment of Pine Alpha (upper plot) compared to the master chronology (lower plot). "Missing" rings are circled - see the text.

Published Data

When major advances in science are made it is customary for sufficient data to be published to allow the scientific community to independently evaluate the conclusions reached. Considering the farreaching implications of the bristlecone pine chronology to radiocarbon dating, archaeology, climatology, etc., one would expect generous documentation of the basic chronology. Actually, apart from the Pine Alpha data discussed above, no ring width data have been published for the components of the chronology.

Briefly, there is information on which samples go where in the chronology, how sensitive the samples are, but not how well they fit, i.e., the correlation between one sample and another. Since no ring width data is available it is not possible to independently check the published conclusions. Requests to obtain such data have met with refusal:

1. Dendrochronology has been shown to be on solid scientific footing with successful applications in several fields of investigation.
2. The bristlecone pine chronology has been reviewed and reasons found to ask the following questions:
   (a) How can such a chronology be constructed with a high percentage of complacent specimens?
   (b) How can specimens with up to 10 percent of their rings missing be cross matched under any circumstances?
   (c) How can this chronology be used to "calibrate" radiocarbon dating when radiocarbon dating is used in construction of the chronology?
   (d) If a ring is "missing" how can it be found, especially when a high percentage of rings are missing?
   (e) Why is only the final chronology published, with refusal to release the data upon which it is based?

It is concluded that at this time there are no compelling reasons to accept the bristlecone pine chronology as valid.

DENDROCHRONOLOGICAL DATA ANALYSIS

One of indirect indicators of climate change under effect natural and anthropogenic factors is width of a radial increment of year tree rings. Dendrochronology (dendroindication) of natural and anthropogenic changes of the nature promotes analysis of a conditions and dynamics of geocomplexes at the retrospective and can be used for the forecasts. The estimation of relationships between dendrochronologic and climatic indexes creates the basis for renovation of elements of a climate for the period determined by age of tree-ring-type chronologies. Rather short duration of the hydrometeorological time series and the features of spatial distribution of the weather stations allow making analysis only for processes and phenomena, restricted by relatively short time-space scales. The region for investigations occupy of the Eastern Fennoscandia including taiga sub-zones of the Kola Peninsula, Karelia, Vologda and Arkhangelsk regiones.

The dating of natural processes and phenomena, anthropogenic effects on the nature, historical events implements with using the dendrochronological scales. The main advantage of tree-ring method is in obtaining relatively long series of observations. Material for our dendrochronologic researches are: a pine *Pinus sylvestris* L., a fir-tree of European (*Picea abies* (L.) Karst.) and Siberian (*Picea abovata* Ledeb.) species, a Siberian larch (*Larix sibirica* Ledeb.), and a juniper *Juniperus communis* L.

The samples were taken by Pressler's age bore with a working section 45 cm. In exeptional cases the disks were carved. For review and scoring of tree-rings a binocular microskope was used. The annual increments of tree rings was calculated with accuracy in 0,05 mm. The measurements of arboreal discs were made on two radiuses - from centre punches on perpendicular lines of tree-rings.

The dendrochronologic samples were taken during the field expeditions at the period from 1995 till 1999 at Karelia, Arkhangelsk, Vologda and Murmansk districts from the living trees and from historical and mineral (fossil) arbors, and the sites, where the samples were collected.

For interpretation obtained dendrochronologic time series the standardizing of the natural data was applied. It is necessary for equalization of the physiologically conditioned differences of the natural data, i. e. for reduction them to indexes.

An optimal method for computation of tree-ring indexes is the calculation by technique of a "corridor", offered by S. Shijatov (1986). In accordance to this method on the diagram of tree-ring series two curves are marking: on the most maximum and minimum values. At calculation of indexes of increment the attitude of points within the limit of a "corridor" take into account. The transformed in accordance of method of a "corridor", and tree-ring diagram transformed in accordance to the method of a "corridor".

For simplification of calculations, width of a corridor was taken equal 100 or 200% (in last case the values of indexes changes from 0 to 200%). For calculation of indices, the following equation was used:

$$I = 100[(L_f - L_{min})/(L_{max} - L_{min})],$$

or, respectively

$$I = 200[(L_f - L_{min})/(L_{max} - L_{min})],$$

where I is index of increment, per cent; L_f is width of a year ring, L_{min} is difference between an abscissa axis and minimum curve, L_{max} is difference between an abscissa and maximum curve.

Advantages of this method are:

- visualization and capability of validation of sampling of models;
- possibility to reveal not only short-term, but also long-term climatically conditioned oscillations in tree-ring series;
- an absence of a non-homogeneous in tree-ring serie
- the duration of initial time series is not reduced.

The indexing of absolute numbers of sampled dendrochronologic time series on a method of a "corridor" was make with application of a software "Indexa. V. 08/99". Obtained series were tested with using statistical methods (trend, spectral, regression, auto- and cross-correlation analysis, etc.) with using of a computer statistical program. The method of cross-dating was applied for more accurate definition of the characteristics of dendrochronological series, received for the groups of samples, taken from one locations. First of all for the cross analysis served the samples, taken from the oldest trees, and from historical wooden facilities and mineral timbers. This samples were collected from architectural constructions, the data building which one are approximately known under the archive data. Some samples of mineral timber were obtained at historical corduroy road "Osudareva doroga", which was built at 1702.

In a process of our study the basic principles of dendrochronological researches (principle of monotony, principle of limiting factor, principle of ecological valence etc.) were applied.

For the creation of temporary scales of a increment of tree-year rings of different localities of territory of the studied area were used the representative dendrochronologic time series (models) obtained from unimpaired alive arbors of different age. The indexes of each model were mated in generalized series, which one were finally built by more continuous tree-ring series. Cross-dating of the models with mineral and historical timber did allowed in some cases to prolong the scales on 100-200 years and more. The duration of the scales is changed from 187 to 488 years.

Accommodation of the obtained arboreal chronologies in a southern part of Karelia, in a middle taiga sub-zone of softwood forests, gave possibility to generalize indexes of the local scales into unified time series of increment of tree-rings. For the territories of the north of Karelia and for the Kola Peninsula the local unified three-ring type chronologies were created too. Obtained local dendrochronological scales were analyzed on the separate years and periods in the comparison with the hydrometeorological data of instrument observations on the climate stations, located in Karelia (Petrozavodsk, Olonets, Sortavala, Loukhi and Kestenga), and with the instrumental data on the water level regime of Lake Onega, as will be show at next chat of the report.

By result of the analysis of the tree-ring data in Finland, it was obtained that in a pine (*Pinus sylvestris* L.) the variations of the contents of an isotope of carbon ^{14}C most intimately correlate with summer air temperature in a vegetation period. The correlation coefficients between mean month temperature and concentration of CO_2 in tree-rings for the Northern Finland are the highest for July and August, during the period of the maximum growth of the trees.

It is established that the activity of growth depends on a course of annual air temperature. The matching of indexes of dendrochronological scales obtain from a pine (*Pinus sylvestris* L.) on both territories Southern Karelia and Southern Finland (Zetterberg, 1990a) demonstrates some resemblance of processes of a increment of annual tree-rings of a pine in adjacent areas.

On these diagrams the period of large amplitudes of timber increment marked in XVI-XVIII centuries is well excreted. Extremely unfavorable for growth of a pine in a middle taiga zone of Karelia and Finland were 1590 and 1640 decades. From a beginning XIX century the amplitude of accretions is decrease, that can be a consequent of the total tendency on warming during final stage of a "small drift epoch". In accordance to instrumental observations, the maximum annual air temperature in Karelia and Finland was marked in 1990 decades of present century. Positive trend in increasing of annual precipitation also was marked. The rather cold period was observed from middle 1950 up to middle 1970 decades, that is in a good correspondence with the dendrochronological data, obtained in our researches.

TaComparison of dendrochronological scales of a middle taiga zones both of Middle Ural (Shijatov, 1986) and Southern Karelia have shown the high synchronism and synphasic of descending changes in tree-rings increment of pines, located on the big distance (thousand kilometers and more) from each other. The coefficient of linear correlation between this two time series is not high (r = 0,3), however qualitative resemblance of this curves indicates a manifested coincidence of processes, which one exerted influence on change of tree-ring increment, apparently, having climatic components.

Thus, it is possible to approve that during the 450-year period the climatic processes in the territory of northern-west part of Russia, down to Ural, wore synchronic nature. Both on Middle Ural, and in Eastern Fennoscandia operating one limiting factor does not show, a composit complex of climatic factors are influence on increment of tree-rings, and first of all are mean air temperature and precipitation during the vegetation period of year.

Characteristic of a radial increment of woody plants growing in different parts of taiga forests is the availability of enough regular and well fixed perennial oscillations of different duration. In the majority dendrochronologic time series obtained in our researches, there are some cycles of different duration, which one being imposed against each other, extremely complicate their selection and interpretation. For construction of dendrochronologic time series in the present investigation the arbors age per 150-350 years were used. Therefore only cycles with duration not more than few decades were reliable estimated. The obtained indexes were subjected to a statistical analysis in comparison to time series of air temperature (May-August), instrumentally obtained on the 5 climate stations (Petrozavodsk, Olonets, Sortavala, Loukhi and Kestenga).

The correlation analysis shows that there is a gentle climate signal in the series of year increment of timber. The correlation coefficients are in the interval from r = 0.20 up to r = 0.35. The different models of time smoothing were applied with the smoothing periods at 3, 5, 7, 11, 21, and 31 years. Thus the correlation coefficients was increased up to r = 0.48 v 0.53. Nevertheless, the visual analyses shows a matched course of the 5-year smoothed diagrams both dendrochronologic time series and series of the air temperature for the warm period of year, coefficient of synchronism thus reaches 0.75.

The stationarity of generalized dendrochronologic time series for the territory of Eastern Fennoscandia and air temperature time series for the climate station Petrozavodsk was estimated with using the auto-correlation function. The fluctuations of these function show clearly, the auto-correlation function long dces not dump, that confirms the quasiperiodic nature of the oscillations. Thus, the process of increment of timber for the studied area is steady enough, each value of annual increment correlates with previous, at least, with a correlation coefficient r = 0.75, and it is possible to made conclusion about enough high degree of predictability of process.

With the purpose of detection of relationship between both air temperature and tree-ring increment time series, and for the determination of possible common cycles their mutual correlation analysis was make also. The spectral analysis and the reciprocal relationship in frequency area with using of the function of coherency and phase difference estimation of the time series were made. The resemblance in long-term changes of tree-ring-type chronologies and air temperature for the warm period of year in the studied territory shows in a spectral density analysis, which one demonstrates significant cyclic changes in a increment of timber with duration about 40 and 13 years and significant of mean temperature for May-August on the same frequencies.

The contribution of these oscillation makes about 35-40 per cent in a dispersion of a increment of timber and air temperature accordingly. The smaller conterminous are marked also in the field of frequencies conforming to time scales about 19-22 years and about 5-7 years. In a spectrum of tree-ring time series the peaks of frequencies in the field corresponds to 9-11 years are visible also. The greatest values the coefficient of coherence of two parsed spectra reached in area of 19-22 years oscillations, the 13-year cycles are less significant.

The well-marked peaks in spectra corresponds to 40-year quasiperiodic oscillations. In spectra of other chronologies, obtained for Southern Karelia, the periods about 11, 13, 18, 22, and 29-30 years are present. Close to century and century oscillations were estimated only for tree-ring chronologies, which one have age more than 300 years. However century cycles for the majority of old-age pine timbers are not always fixed. Only in separate dendrochronologic series of a middle taiga zone of the Eastern Fennoscandia the cycles closed to 110-year were found. This cycles can be united from two 50-year cycles. Some cycles with the super-century duration are marked in the studied area also.

The cycle with duration about 4750 years found in the select dendrochronologies of the taiga sub-zone of Eastern Fennoscandia also described for the Ural sub-region of Polar, sub-Polar and Southern Ural. This cycle, closed by 3035 years, usually concerns to the so-call Brickner cycle. The cycle with duration about 2122 years most often meets in oscillations of tree-ring increment and detecting of this cycle in geophusical and biological phenomena the majority of investigators connect to reacting to the conforming oscillations of solar activity. The cycles, detected in our researches, coincide the data for the northern and southern sub-zones of taiga of the Eastern Fennoscandia. As result of application of a method of auto-correlation for analysis of tree-ring dendrochronologies of studied area the next conclusions were made:

- the stationarity in oscillations of dendrochronologic scales depends on a degree of extremeness of conditions of a habitation and effect of the exogenic factors.
- at decomposing of the obtained frequencies of the dendroscales on time of their development it is possible to mark, that the cycles within periods of 11-22 years dominate at the end of XVIII and at the first half of XIX c. At the end of XIX and beginning of XX centuries there is a rearrangement of oscillations of tree-ring increment to the side of more high 5-7 years cycles.
- at XX century the oscillations close to century and century duration strengthen.

Thus, because the described cycles meet in the majority of obtained dendrochronologies, it is possible with a large degree of probability to suspect, that all called cycles have exogenic nature. But it is very difficult to observe all links of solar-earth relationships, and it is possible only to state their influence on the timber increment. The qualitative comparison of a solar activity (presented by Wolf's numbers) and tree-ring increment time series for the period from 1700 up to 1984 years was made also. Visually it is possible to mark noticeable resemblance of a radial increment of year rings of obtained time series and oscillations of a solar activity.

For a quantitative estimation of the relationship the correlation coefficients were calculated, which one equals from 0.32 up to 0.50 for different cases, both without smoothing and for smoothed time series. Thus, the relationships between a solar activity and tree-ring increment shows quantitative not clearly.

Data analysis of dendrochronologic time series showed that the tendencies of climate variability may be defined at the level of internal to century cycles. The present researches allow to made a conclusion about existing quasiperiodic variations of climate. Probably, there is a dependence of tree-ring increment from joint influence of climatic factors (air temperature for the warm period of year, temperature and humidity of soil, precipitation etc.). It is not obviously possible yet to select of one universal factor clearly influencing on the radial increment of trees in investigated territory.

For detection of dynamics of the natural and anthropogenic processes at inshore geocomplexes of the largest water bodies of the studied territory the fieldworks for collecting and testing tree-ring samples of a pine (*Pinus sylvestris* L.) and a fir-tree (*Picea abies* L.) growing near to Lake Onega were make at 1997-1999 years. From all this samples, selected in inshore complexes, including insular, 108 samples were selected for analysis.

The dendroindication of the samples in comparison with the water level dynamic of Lake Onega did showed that years with the maxima of increment of tree-rings of arbors, growing nearby the lake, are in accordance to the years with the high average water level (1888, 1889, 1894, 1910, 1924, 1936, 1946, 1955, 1958, 1962, 1977, 1979, 1984, 1988). The years of minimum accretions coincide with years of minimum horizons of water level (1883, 1891, 1908, 1914, 1921, 1928, 1934, 1940, 1945, 1947, 1948, 1951, 1956, 1960, 1965, 1972, 1980, 1985, 1986, 1990). It is necessary to note, that coincide not only years of extremes in both tree-ring and water level oscillations, but also amplitudes of these changes.

The considerable increase of a water level conducts to the greater increment of tree-ring, as well as decrease of water horizons produced a reverse reaction of a model arbor. For example, in 1940 the lowest value of water level of Lake Onega was marked, and per the same year the most thin ring (0.15 mm) for a model arbor was marked, the mean increment for the long-term period for this time series was 1.37 mm.

Having compared the diagrams of water level and increment of tree-rings, we have marked the fact of coincidence of oscillations during period of a natural water regime of Lake Onega, as well as after 1952, when the Svir hydroelectric power station in the outflow of Svir river was built, and natural regime of the lake was changed. Since1956 the oscillations of water level became less, and since the same year the notably reduction of amplitude increment of tree-ring is marked. The resemblance of a model diagrams is watched for arbors growing in inshore geocomplexes, remote from each other on 50-100 km.

The matching of oscillations of year tree-rings increment of arbors growing in immediate locality from water, with level variation give possibility to restore the level regime for the period from which the instrumental water level observations are absent. The woody plants settle on pebbly barrier beaches in 10-15 years after their formation. A closed-grained substratum, sand and loam soils populate by arbors usually within 2-5 years.

Therefore, after analysis samples taken at the inshore zone of Lake Onega, we have received following conclusions : the maiden barrier beach of the lake was derivated in 1825-1828, the average water level in this period was, in interquartile, on 0, 4-0, 5 m higher, than modern; the second barrier beach, adjusted for an initial increment of timber, was formed in the beginning 1520 years. Therefore, the average water level of Lake Onega at this period was even higher on 1, 5-2, 0 m. The variations of water level in the different parts of the lake are concordanced and both time of formation of barrier beaches and altitudes of a water per elapsed centuries are corresponds to them.

He has obtained, that during XIV-XVI centuries the long-time increasing of the common moistening, at least, in the Northern hemisphere, was marked. In this period in a water areas of the Baltic sea and other large water bodies the often strong gales blasting piers reconfiguring shore lines were characteristic. The forming of powerful barrier beaches around Lake Onega, which has been dated by us as formed at 20-30 decades of XVI century, is connected, is most interquartile, with strong gales of the given epoch. These barrier beaches are specially great in south-east part of a lake, where their relative altitudes makes about 2-2,5 m. The outcomes about the long-term changes of a precede regime of Lake Onega, obtained with using of dendrochronologic method.

Conclusion

The joint analysis of dendro- and climatical series has shown that in increment of timber in the Eastern Fennoscandia there is a relation with climatic and other geophysical factors. However, universal exogenic effect producing an enough strong mating signal in variability of width tree rings for taiga sub-zones of studied territory in not revealed. It is necessary to note that temperature of the warm period of year (June-August) exerts the most significant influence on oscillation of growth of pine timber stands in different sites of Karelia and southern part of the Kola Peninsula. Besides, the relationship between an increment of annual rings and solar activity variations is detected, which one, probably, influences on growth of a wooden plants indirectly.

In dendrochronologic series of a sub-zone of northern taiga the noticable displacement of a cyclicity in low frequency band is observed, and the cycles with duration at 30-35 and 110 years are detected. Secular cycles in regions of northern limits of a lignosa propagation are marked in tree-ring chronologies of the Taimyr, Polar Ural, Ural-Siberian sub-Arctic, Middle Siberia and others.

In the most chronologies of middle taiga, 40-, 19-22-, 13-, 9-11-, and 5-7-year cycles are found, the nature of which one is conditioned, in all probability, by oscillations of mean air temperature for May-August, because their periods are characteristic for cycles of both temperature meteorological and solar activity time series. However, for stands of trees of a taiga zone of the Eastern Fennoscandia the applicability of dendrochronologic forecasts of meteorological elements is possible while only at a level of an estimation of the tendencies and qualitative changes.

The joint analysis of indirect indicators of climate changes gives the basis to suppose, that the existence of "small ice drift epoch" or "stage of Fernay" in the Eastern Fennoscandia at XIV-XIX centuries also took place. In this period there was a cooling-down and humidifying of a climate, that was result to increasing of total moistening and rising of water levels of lakes, in particular Lake Onega.

The coupled analysis of dendrochronological and climatic series has shown that there is a relationship between climatic and other geophysical factors in increment of timber in the Eastern Fennoscandia. However, the universal exogenic effect producing the strong mating signal in the width of tree rings for taiga sub-zones of studied territory is not revealed for the territory of Karelia.

The use of tree-ring dating has increased rapidly over the last two decades, and enough results have now been published to undertake an assessment of what has been learnt, to review the present position, and to consider future directions. The paper seeks to identify a number of issues currently concerning both dendrochronologists and those who use the data. The benefits of accurate dating are considerable. Precise dates are not only important for understanding individual buildings, but are leading to the reassessment of both regional chronologies and the development of construction and technique. It is suggested that we may now be in a position to start identifying general trends in the incidence of buildings of different types and status over the country as a whole. At present this kind of analysis can only be tentative, but in the long run it will enable us to place buildings in a wider historical context, and help us to cross the chasm between documentary historians and those who study buildings.

THE TECHNIQUE OF TREE RING DATING

Tree ring dating is a technique with which most of us are now familiar, whether or not we have been in a position to use it and benefit from the results. Dates for British buildings have been published annually in *Vernacular Architecture* since 1980, and have also appeared elsewhere. Enough has now been done for an attempt to be made to assess what has been learnt so far, to review current concerns and to make suggestions for the future.

In 1984 an unpublished report on dendrochronology to the CBA Historic Building Committee noted that over the previous fifteen years tree-ring curves had been established for several areas of the British Isles, and over 100 buildings or parts of buildings had been dated. However, much more needed to be done. At that time no curves had been successfully established for the south west, the south east, or East Anglia. Work by the laboratories had largely concentrated on three issues: on the statistical theory of sampling, the verification of the basic method, and the establishment of model curves. Very little sampling had then been undertaken for the purpose of architectural dating, and at that time only RCHME seemed likely to be in a position to commission such work. In addition, the collection of samples was not always combined with rigorous examination of the structures from which they were taken, which invalidated some of the results, while publication of those results was often inadequate.

While things can no doubt still be improved, we have certainly come a long way in the last thirteen years. Curves have been established for new areas and dates for 650 or more buildings have been listed in *Vernacular Architecture* alone - although it has to be said that others have not yet appeared. Rigorous correlation of samples and structures is increasingly taken as a matter of course, published results are far more informative, and the technique is starting to become available as a tool for building recorders of all kinds. It is used to advance knowledge of both individual structures and groups of buildings and, perhaps most importantly of all, is beginning to further our understanding of wider historical questions.

Many buildings have been selected on an individual basis, but since the mid 1980s a number of large-scale projects have got underway. Of these, only the conclusions for RCHME in Kent, and for RCAHMW in Wales, have yet been published, although papers have been delivered based on the work of the Leverhulme cruck project in the Midlands, the Shropshire dendrochronological project, and the RCHME northern roofs project, and the dates of the individual buildings from these projects have been published in *Vernacular Architecture*. Without a full understanding of each area and its buildings, or of what was in the minds of those who commissioned the work, this wealth of material can only be given very summary treatment; it is too soon to draw firm conclusions. What follows is a preliminary and tentative assessment, indicating potentially interesting advances, which will require further research to substantiate. This paper concentrates on work on vernacular buildings, and does not discuss the results of important work on ecclesiastical roofs, particularly on the roofs of cathedrals.

The possibility of having precise dates for the timbers of standing strucures is a heady inducement to building recorders to seek the help of dendrochronology in interpreting their material. But obtaining precise dates is not always simple. There are a number of reaso why timbers will not date, some of which are in the process of being overcome, but some of which may remain recalcitant. Before discussing the results published so far, it is wrth looking at some of the problems which can be encountered.

As the discussion of geographical coverage suggests, climatic coditions mean that it has proved very difficult in certain parts of the British Isles to establish the local master chronologies thathe south west and East Anglia has been notoriously difficult, although progress is now being made. In these areas local climate patterns, or possibly the effects of woodland management, mean that the way forward may be through producing local chronologies for relatively small regions, and building outwards from them. This was the case in Essex where the breakthrough came from intensely detailed work on the Cressing Temple site; and in Devon, where work has concentrated on a small area north of Crediton. Another very localised 'ecological niche' has been recognised around Durham.

Dating is done by cross-matching, or correlating, the pattern of ring-growth in a particular tree with a previously established master curve, possibly obtained from trees in another area. The quality of match is expressed in terms of 't-values', with high t-values - say at least 5 - giving more cause for confidence in the date than low ones. Most people are aware that a certain number of rings are necessary in order to obtain a reliable date. However, there is some disagreement among dendrochronologists as to what the smallest number of rings may be for a reliable match. Some believe that 80 or more rings of surviving annual growth are required for a result; others that reliable results can be got from as few as 50 rings. In some places trees grew so fast that timbers were used which have far fewer than 50 rings surviving, and at present such timbers are unlikely to date. The question of whether such trees can be dated is one which is currently being debated and researched by the professionals. Those whose background lies in statistics take a more positive view of the potential for success than those who are primarily archaeologists or natural scientists. Such discussions are beyond the sphere of most clients but, since they can affect the results, it is useful to know that they are taking place.

One problem that is being encountered is that in some regions, timbers of certain periods simply will not date. As the results published in *Vernacular Architecture* indicate, a relatively large number of late thirteenth and early fourteenth-century buildings have been dated from many parts of England. But not from Kent. In that county buildings which are almost certainly of this period have so far proved to be undateable, even when there are a considerable number of rings . Similar situations occur elsewhere. In part the answers may be related to climate, but there are also theories that it may be due to woodland management. The problem does not concern the period of felling, but rather the period when the trees germinated. A twelfth-century gap in the germination date of trees in the Midlands has led the Nottingham laboratory to set up a project specifically to examine Sherwood Forest oak In other laboratories the same issues are being looked at during the course of other work. It has also been suggested that the way trees were grown in the fourteenth century affected the quality and availability of fast-grown timber in the first half of the fifteenth century, although the last section of this paper suggests that social and economic explanations may also be likely causes for a relative dearth of certain types of standing buildings in this particular period. However, the whole question of the way trees were grown is one which is directly relevant to all dendrochronology. Some research has already been undertaken on cross-matching timbers from living trees, where ecological and genetic variations can be studied in a controlled manner. When more research has been done the results are likely to be of considerable significance for those who study standing structures.

Further complications arise in regions where much of the building timber was elm or other wood. Elm was frequently used in Somerset in both medieval and later buildings; it was used in medieval buildings in Warwickshire and in parts of Kent, notably in the north east of the county where timber was scarcer, and after the Middle Ages is found in abundance in the Cotswolds, the Chilterns and parts of the Midlands. As yet, chronologies have only been established for oak, and there are differing views as to whether these can be used for dating elm, which anyway tends to be fast grown and to have 'complacent' ring patterns which are less easy to date. Several laboratories are looking into the problems associated with dating both elm and beech, and English Heritage is currently funding work on conifers, which will be relevant primarily to post-medieval buildings. So far, in some areas samples from other types of tree have cross-matched with oak, while elsewhere they have not. Thus the dating of timber other than oak is a subject for future research.

A good match with a high t-value against a local master will date all the rings present in the timber, and in particular will give the date of its last ring. However, this last ring may not be the last ring of the tree from which it came, since some of the soft, outer, sapwood rings may have been removed by the carpenter or lost over the years. The felling date of timbers which have bark remaining can be precisely ascertained, whereas the felling dates of those which have only sapwood, or the heartwood/sapwood boundary, can only be given an approximate date, the degree of certainty depending upon the number of sapwood rings remaining and the accuracy with which the likely number of sapwood rings has been calculated. Current estimates of these vary, with some researchers proposing that it is 95% certain that sapwood rings range between 10 and 55 per tree, and others that there are more likely to be between 15 and 50 sapwood rings. The question of estimation, and the presentation of such results for public consumption, is discussed in more detail in Dan Miles's paper below. It is important because estimated felling dates are usually clear guides to construction dates, and are therefore critical to the analysis of the results of the last few years.

The situation is further complicated by the fact that trees do not all have the same average number of sapwood rings. In certain areas, in Brittany for example, and in Kent, it has been shown that there were fewer than in some other regions. Calculation of the number, and therefore estimation of the felling dates of timbers, may need to be refined as work in an area proceeds. This is precisely what occurred in Kent. At the start of that project the number of sapwood rings in trees was estimated as thirty, within a range of fifteen to fifty for 95% of all mature trees (30, -15 + 20). By the end of the project, the evidence from firmly dated timbers suggested that the number should be revised to twenty five, within a range of fifteen to thirty five (25, -/+10). The effect was to pull all the estimated dates back by 5 years. If one is going in for accurate dating, this matters. In the meantime the earlier dates had been published and may well be inaccurately repeated (not surprisingly, they crept into the first draft of the database used in the preparation of this article). In Brittany, two sets of sapwood estimates have been calculated, the first on the basis of the historical material, the second using good evidence from modern trees. Dates calculated by each method are different, and the dendrochronologists are reluctant to throw their weight wholly behind one set or the other . It is likely that as more work is done, local variations will increasingly be recognised and taken into account when dates are calculated.

One view is that where felling dates are not precise, that is, where bark or evidence of bark is not present on a sample, only date ranges should be given. But even then people may, for the purposes of calculation, turn that range into a single, notional date in order to create tables of the sort illustrated later in this article. Since the most likely felling date does not necessarily lie in the centre of the range, calculations made by the ignorant will be less accurate than calculations made by the professionals themselves. These are tricky issues which are currently engaging the attention of dendrochronologists. Those for whom dates matter need to be aware that there are very real problems to be resolved, and our eagerness to accept precise dates which may not be correct is a worrying concern.

GEOGRAPHICAL AND CHRONOLOGICAL COVERAGE

Large-scale projects and individual sampling have between them covered considerable parts of the country but, there are still areas of Britain where few results have so far been obtained.

Hardly any buildings have yet been dated on the west coast, from Scotland to Lands End. Although not shown on this map, this lacunae extends also to the Channel Islands, where only one building has so far proved dateable . The situation in the west is improving, but still has a long way to go. Much of the dating in eastern Wales and Shropshire has taken place in the last three or four years, successful sampling in Cornwall and Somerset has only really begun in the last two, and the Sheffield laboratory is currently devoting considerable effort to building a chronology for Devon. The situation on the eastern coast of England is much the same. Very little work has been done successfully in the north east, although this has recently begun to be rectified through projects devoted to truncated principal roof. Further south, little has taken place in Lincolnshire, other than in Lincoln itself, while in East Anglia less than half a dozen buildings have been dated in Norfolk and Suffolk. Although a number of results have recently been obtained in western Essex , the prevalence of timber-framed buildings in that part of the country means there is obviously a great deal more to be learnt.

In the early stages, in order to establish local chronologies, it may be important to get buildings dated, no matter what kind of buildings they are So the first buildings to be dated in a region are often of limited value in sorting out architectural chronology. As more buildings are dated, dating becomes easier, and the selection can be more refined. But as long as the number of buildings dated in the whole of the British Isles remains limited, there are bound to be biases. Work has been funded by researchers with specific questions in mind, and their attention has frequently been directed to buildings of a particular type or date. This has produced a preponderance of dated crucks in the Midlands, of a particular roof type in the northern counties, of early barns in Essex, and of rural medieval houses in Kent. To the results of these and other projects can be added a growing number of results from 'one-off' sites, which are making a welcome extension of coverage to buildings of all kinds and dates. Nonetheless, anyone using the published dates needs to be aware of the biases that are presently built into them.

There are a number of reasons for this. Firstly, the desire to sort out the early chronology of timber-framed construction, eg. aisled and base cruck buildings, has led to a concentration of effort on the earliest surviving structures. The fact that buildings of the twelfth, thirteenth and fourteenth centuries are, relatively speaking, extremely well-represented on the maps, is due to this research aim. Secondly, the large-scale research projects which have used dendrochronology have almost all been concerned with medieval themes. This is hardly surprising, for it is clear that the value of tree-ring dating in the Middle Ages, when documents, date stones and stylistic detail are scarce, can hardly be over estimated. For the first time ever, researchers have the ability to date their subjects with some confidence. It is noticeable that the majority of seventeenth and eighteenth-century dates are clustered in parts of the north east Midlands where more work has been initiated and funded by local authorities, whose agendas are perhaps not confined to pure historical research. Finally, medieval buildings were largely built with virgin timber, whereas later buildings often reused earlier material, which means that successful tree-ring dating of later buildings may be more patchy.

THE DATING OF INDIVIDUAL BUILDINGS

In a number of cases dendrochronological dates have been found to coincide very closely with documented dates for building. Such confirmation of the accuracy of the technique is immensely reassuring for all who use tree-ring dates. A good match occurred, for example, at the Abbots House, Shrewsbury, where precise felling dates of 1457 and 1458 were obtained, and in 1459 a building ceremony was recorded, attended by the Abbot of Lilleshall, his carpenter and borough officials. In Hampshire, the barn of Overton Court, belonging to the Bishop of Winchester, was erected with timber felled in 1496, while the house was built with timber felled in 1496, 1504 and 1505. These dates gave the researcher, Edward Roberts, an indication of where to search in the accounts, leading to the discovery that timber was acquired both in 1496/7 and in 1505/6, while the building of the barn and house were respectively documented in 1497/8 and 1506/7 . This is one of several instances in Hampshire where tree-ring dating facilitated documentary research, leading to significant advances in understanding the buildings.

Even when timbers have been more tentatively dated than in these cases, they can tie in well with documentary evidence. In Canterbury, it is known that the Sun Inn in Burgate was under construction in 1437-8 . Tree-ring dating provided no precise date, but a range of 1425-60, later revised to 1425-45. Within the range the most likely felling date was first estimated as *c*1440, later as *c*1435. The date ranges encompassed the documented date, and both the estimated dates within the ranges were close, but it is somewhat heartening to find that the revision brought it to what must be about the most probable felling date on grounds other than dendrochronology. This kind of evidence inevitably gives the user confidence in the methods of estimation.

Dating of individual structures, often undertaken as part of the restoration programme of large and important buildings, has contributed significantly to the understanding of those buildings, and often enabled them to be placed more accurately in a wider context. Many of these projects have been funded by the owners of the sites, or by English Heritage, Cadw or local authorities. The contribution official bodies have made to the understanding of the buildings in their care, or upon which they are giving advice, is considerable. In Nottinghamshire, for example, relevant buildings are now recorded and tree-ring dated as a regular part of County Council conservation casework. The results often lead to a building being upgraded, and therefore eligible for grant aid. They have contributed to an increased understanding of the county's heritage, which is of considerable value to conservation officers as well as to historians, and they have helped to interest the general public in historic buildings, often raising funds for restoration in the process.

An early but notable result from sampling individual buildings with the help of local organisations came through work on the timbers of the great hall in Leicester Castle, whose structural history was complex and ill-understood Although no precise date for the early work was obtained, due to the absence of sapwood, it became clear that the original aisled hall was built in the twelfth century but was wholly reconstructed in the sixteenth century, retaining only the arcade posts. The revised comprehension of the structure made it possible to place the hall in the milieu of other early halls, such as those at the Bishop's Palace, Hereford, and Burmington Manor and Temple Balsall in Warwickshire. All these buildings have now been tree-ring dated, with greater or less degrees of precision, and gradually our understanding of the development of these early buildings is advancing.

Tree-ring dating has likewise helped to clarify complex situations in later buildings whose dates were the subject of debate, and sometimes also to pinpoint the likely builders. Examples are Gainsborough Old Hall in Lincolnshire, of the 1460s and 1480s, Oakwell House, Birstall, in West Yorkshire, of the 1580s, and parts of Daneway House, Bisley, in Gloucestershire, of 1674, where a conflict of views over the dates of plasterwork and panelling was resolved by dating the timberwork . In some cases tree-ring dating has simplified what appeared to be a complex sequence of building; so that what was thought, on structural evidence, to be of two dates, has been shown to be of one, even if constructed in two phases. Charlton Court Barn, Steyning, in West Sussex, of 1404-6, and Tickenham Court, Clevedon, in Avon, of 1471-6 are both examples of this. In other cases, as in the former infirmary of Wherwell Abbey in Hampshire, what had been assumed to be one phase turned out to be two. While dating major buildings is valuable in terms of the immediate work in hand, the results also contribute to our general understanding of architectural development. This cumulative effect will become increasingly apparent as time goes by.

A recent development in the application of tree-ring dating has been the sampling of small features, such as partition staves. Small timbers often have as many, or even more, rings than larger ones, and at Three Chimneys in Mapledurham the question of whether a partition was original or not was resolved in this manner. Another potentially important development is measurement by specialised photography. This has been used for some time for prepared end grain; but the reading of rings from a radial section on the *face* of a plank or beam is now being explored, for example at Stokesay Castle. At the moment such work is very experimental, but if it can be developed further, then it may become possible to date important parts of buildings which cannot be cored in the normal manner.

Nearly everyone who has experience of tree-ring dating will have found themselves in for some surprises. Buildings which one felt reasonably confident in dating, turn out to be later or earlier than expected. With a single building it may be difficult to turn this new knowledge to constructive use, but with a group of buildings it can affect one's picture of chronological development and enable one to look at one's material in a new way. It is perhaps invidious to pick out examples, for the phenomenon is widespread. Certainly, in my work in Kent I initially made mistakes in dating, and learnt a great deal from being able to initiate a substantial tree-ring dating programme which allowed the construction of a framework for dating buildings throughout the Middle Ages. As a former member of the RCHME Threatened Buildings team I, like my more illustrious seniors, was a late dater. This no doubt arose from the experience of working across England, of knowing a little about many areas, but few areas in depth. An example from Kent is Clakkers Hall, Plaxtol, published in *English Vernacular Houses* as *c*1500, but now known to be built of timbers felled between 1442 and 1462, with a likely felling date of *c*1452.

One interesting point to emerge from the lists in *Vernacular Architecture* is that a number of urban buildings, once thought to date from the fifteenth century, were built of timber felled at a much earlier period. The Cross Keys Inn, Leicester, dates from after 1309, probably *c*1334 , while 'Severns', formerly in Middle Pavement, Nottingham, is now firmly dated to 1335. Assuming the buildings were erected shortly after the felling dates, these are substantial and significant revisions, and the whole question of urban dates will be touched upon again in a later section of this paper. A look at the lists also indicates that larger buildings in Shropshire have produced some unexpected dates. On the one hand, the Prior's Hall in Much Wenlock, generally considered to date from *c*1500, has been shown to have been erected with timbers felled in 1425. On the other, some earlier halls such as Upton Cressett Hall and Moat House, Longnor, previously thought to date from the late fourteenth century, are now known to have been built with timbers felled only in the second and third quarters of the fifteenth century. Thus the timbers of buildings which had been considered to be a hundred years apart were in fact felled at more or less the same time, and the sequence of their dates has even been reversed. Whether the felling date for the timbers of the Prior's Hall is the date of building may be another question, and the conclusions of the researchers must be awaited with interest. If so, this kind of redating may lead to a new view of the development of medieval building in the county. Shropshire is one of the few counties where medieval houses of all kinds and of varying status have been sampled systematically, so the conclusions will be particularly valuable. While results of this sort may mean a revision of views on chronological development in some areas, it will be less obvious in regions where attention has focused on a narrower range of building types, and likely to be most marked where research and publication have been going on for a long time. In areas where intensive research is more recent, changes in dates will probably be less dramatic, since the lessons of tree-ring dating, even if applied from results in other regions, are likely to form part of the initial analysis.

It would be wrong to give the impression that all dating is in the melting pot and that all chronologies must be revised. In Shropshire, as elsewhere, tree-ring dating has in many cases confirmed dating done by traditional methods of stylistic and structural analysis. As Christopher Currie remarked recently, after thirty years' research and a tree-ring dating programme in Oxfordshire, his conclusions remain much the same. This does not imply that much of tree-ring dating is a waste of time. On the contrary, the fact that previous dates were obtained by less scientific methods means that it was not possible to treat them with the confidence that dendrochronology inspires. If buildings are to be used to further historical research, then accurate dating is critical, and confirmation of previous dating is just as important as correction.

CONSTRUCTION AND TECHNIQUE

The generally accepted chronological development of early timber-framed structures has been largely confirmed by tree-ring dating, although the tendency has been to push some of the smallest early survivors back in date. However, the results of the only large-scale programmes of tree-ring dating specifically aimed at studying construction: the Leverhulme cruck project in the Midlands and the RCHME truncated principals project in northern England, have not yet been published. Until that time it is not really possible to assess the full implications of what has been learnt from extended programmes of this kind, and a discussion of what dendrochronology has to teach us about structure may be premature.

One important aspect of construction which is likely to be considerably advanced through tree-ring dating is the typology of timber jointing techniques. Pioneered by Cecil Hewett, and based upon his extensive knowledge of early Essex buildings, later augmented by analysis of roofs elsewhere, the evolution of jointing techniques has had a significant effect on the understanding and dating of timber buildings throughout England. While most researchers now accept the broad outlines of Hewett's typology, doubts have been expressed about the detailed chronology and close dating of certain features, and therefore of some buildings. Just as tree-ring dating is clarifying and refining the dating of buildings generally, so it is likely to refine the date ranges of jointing techniques. Since many of the key buildings lie in Essex where dating has proved d One important aspect of construction which is likely to be considerably advanced through tree-ring dating is the typology of timber jointing techniques. Pioneered by Cecil Hewett, and based upon his extensive knowledge of early Essex buildings, later augmented by analysis of roofs elsewhere, the evolution of jointing techniques has had a significant effect on the understanding and dating of timber buildings throughout England. While most researchers now accept the broad outlines of Hewett's typology, doubts have been expressed about the detailed chronology and close dating of certain features, and therefore of some buildings. Just as tree-ring dating is clarifying and refining the dating of buildings generally, so it is likely to refine the date ranges of jointing techniques. Since many of the key buildings lie in Essex where dating has proved difficult, it has not until recently been easy to apply this test. Where results have been obtained, the dates of some in the typological sequence have been confirmed. The dates of the barns at Cressing Temple, for example, are only slightly later than those suggested by Hewett: the first phase of the Barley Barn, previously thought to have been erected in the late twelfth century, is now known to have been constructed between 1205 and 1235, and the earliest phase of the Wheat Barn, previously dated to *c*1255, now dates to *c*1257-80. In both cases the dates have shifted later, although not by any appreciable amount. Other buildings, however, have proved to be considerably later than was originally thought: it is now known that the stave church at Greensted, Essex, and the 'rhenish helm' spire at Sompting church, Sussex, both thought to be pre-Conquest, were built after 1063 and in the early fourteenth century respectively while the earliest phase of the barn at Belchamp St Paul, is not eleventh or twelfth century, but 1240-75 . The importance of redating these and other buildings lies in the fact that they formed part of a closely argued typological sequence with chronological implications, and the redating has reversed the order of some examples. The main outlines of the sequence, which is founded upon detailed knowledge of the structures, is likely to stand, but the longevity of particular jointing forms may make a difference to the chronological profile of the typology. Its importance and influence is such that, when more dates have been obtained, a major re assessment considering the implications of the changes should be undertaken. This will almost certainly improve our perception of the development of medieval construction.

The chronological implications of the typology of aisled halls, base crucks and crucks were never as closely argued; so, while we may learn a great deal about their development and distribution, this is less likely to require a major reassessment of received views on dating. That aisled halls survive from an earlier date than base crucks has long been suggested, and both this and the fact the earliest surviving aisled buildings, dating to the late twelfth or thirteenth centuries, are as likely to lie in the Midlands as in the South East (where they might once have been expected), are confirmed by tree-ring dating . Examples of both·base crucks and crucks date from the middle years of the thirteenth century, with the base cruck at Siddington barn in Gloucestershire dating to 1245-7 , and two cruck blades from Upton Magna in Shropshire producing a date of 1269. These dates are possibly a little earlier than was previously thought, but documentary dates for crucks of some sort, as we have recently been reminded are known from yet earlier in the thirteenth century. In the past it has been suggested that one type of cruck structure developed from the other - different researchers holding different views of the sequence. So far, the earliest dates for the two types are so close that if one developed from the other this must have occurred well before the first surviving examples. Thus, until further analysis is undertaken by those more qualified than the present writer, the question of origins remains as obscure as it was in 1981 Tree-ring dating has, however, confirmed that the bulk of surviving base crucks date to the fourteenth century, while cruck numbers peaked in the mid fifteenth, and continued in some regions throughout the sixteenth. But before any really constructive comments can be made it is essential that the geographical location, function and social status of these structures are considered. The extent to which other aspects of the development of cruck construction, such as the typology of apex forms, have been advanced through the recent dating programme must await publication of the results.

The truncated principal roofs project is concerned with dating a range of roof types which occur in the north, and particularly the north-east, of England between the mid fourteenth and the seventeenth centuries. The earliest examples are combined with crown posts, the later are purely of side-purlin construction. Such roofs are often difficult to date from stylistic evidence, and since they are of varied form, it was thought worthwhile to try and trace their evolution. This has now been achieved, and the results should soon be published . Hopefully, the information will enable roofs of similar construction to be dated more accurately. The roofs are used over buildings of differing type and status, and it seems likely that further advances in knowledge may be made by not only considering the type of roof, but also the status, location and function of the buildings in which the roofs occur. Thus, as in the case of crucks, the initial analysis of results will almost certainly require more contextual research for the full benefits of tree-ring dating to become apparent.

In a number of areas enough work has now been done for comments to be made about what has been discovered. On the whole the results have not been startling, in the sense of overturning previously accepted theories. For this we must be thankful: it is clear that most regional recorders already had a good grasp of typological development, and indeed also of the general outlines of regional chronology. Tree-ring dating has enabled this to be substantiated and refined.

One of the few dramatic findings relates to the work undertaken on agricultural or service buildings belonging to religious estates in and around Durham Seven buildings, which have none of the architectural detail required by traditional methods of dating, have now been tree-ring dated. The result has been to all but double the number of known late-medieval barns in the North East, and provide a framework which may be used to analyse other structures in an area where medieval buildings are rare and extremely difficult to recognise.

In Wales, RCAHMW initiated a programme to date seventeen phases on eleven sites in the north and east of the principality. The aim was to date a range of timber houses, of varying types and social status, between their first appearance and the end of the Middle Ages. The dates fall between the 1430s and the mid sixteenth century (with later dates for inserted ceilings). Not only has a framework been established which will enable local researchers to date other Welsh structures with more confidence, but Welsh buildings can now be compared more readily with dated English ones. For example, base crucks of some distinction were still being constructed there in the mid fifteenth century when they had ceased to be erected in most parts of England; and it is argued that no truly vernacular buildings survive before the mid sixteenth century. The chronological staggering of buildings according to size and social class in Wales is quite striking in contrast to what we know from elsewhere.

In Nottinghamshire, geographical and chronological patterns of dated houses have been published, without regard to size or type of building Sampling has been undertaken on a very wide range of house types and dates within the county, with much of the work having been initiated by an enlightened County Council. It is clear that the earliest houses lie in the south and south east of the county, in the Trent valley and the towns of Nottingham and Newark. The numbers of dated buildings in the larger upland region to the north of the county are both fewer and later. It is likely that this pattern is a true reflection of the surviving buildings on the ground. Perhaps these conclusions were to be expected, but they are none the less welcome, and one suspects that those working in conservation derive major benefits from the increased understanding of the development of timber framing within the county.

Other counties where major programmes are producing results are Derbyshire, Hampshire and Shropshire, while work in Somerset and the Channel Islands is just beginning. The most beneficial results will almost certainly arise in those counties where the sample is taken from the full range of building types, ie. urban and rural, agricultural, domestic and ecclesiastical.

On a smaller scale, Dan Miles is attempting to date the majority of historical structures within the Oxfordshire parish of Mapledurham. Buildings range from the fourteenth to the eighteenth century, and the results, when combined with information from other sources, will add a new dimension to the understanding of the history of the parish.

GENERAL TRENDS SUGGESTED BY THE RESULTS

Tree-ring dates for some 650 buildings have been published so far in *Vernacular Architecture*. Many of the buildings have had more than one phase dated, so that dates for over 800 phases are now known. The lists include cathedrals and churches, monastic ranges, public buildings, houses, both great and small, agricultural buildings, and a few industrial structures. The dates range from the twelfth to the nineteenth centuries, although by far the greatest number fall between the fourteenth and sixteenth centuries. Within this late medieval period there are two noticeable peaks, the first occurs in the early fourteenth century, the second and larger begins in the second half of the fifteenth, reaches a high point by the end of the century, and dies away gradually over the course of the sixteenth century. It may be argued that this chronological pattern of dates indicates little else than the research interests of the clients. Up to a point this must be true since, as discussed above, the technique is most valuable as a research tool for the Middle Ages. But in Shropshire, 62 buildings, comprising 104 phases, have been dated between 1247 and 1666, and a sharp decline in numbers in the first half of the sixteenth century is followed by a marked rise from about 1550. This suggests that the national decline in numbers noted in the sixteenth century may reflect more than just bias on the part of researchers. Elsewhere, not enough later buildings have been sampled for conclusions to be drawn. But for the medieval period as a whole the time may already have come when the body of evidence is large enough to allow a preliminary assessment of the pattern of building.

However, to make sense of trends it is essential to break the buildings down by type or by social status, and this in itself is fraught with ambiguity. Separating houses from barns or churches is simple. Separating greater houses, built by the aristocracy, ecclesiastical institutions or the gentry, from those which may be termed 'vernacular' is far more difficult, particularly since the relevant information may be lacking from the published results. It has, however, been attempted in the following section, which relates only to houses and public buildings. Although some mistakes will have been made, it is hoped that the resulting patterns of building are robust enough to absorb them.

The choice of 33-year intervals is a compromise between the wish to have periods small enough to be significant, but not too small to introduce a spurious sense of accuracy in the case of date ranges or some estimated dates. Where a date range spans two periods, the building has been placed in the period of its estimated date, or, where no estimated date was given, of the centre of the date range. The charts have not been taken beyond 1600 because at present too few later buildings have been dated for any meaningful trends to emerge.

It excludes monastic ranges and royal castles, and also what were obviously town houses, but includes all private residences built by the Crown and by ecclesiastics or ecclesiastical institutions. Clearly, there is a vast difference in status between houses built for the aristocracy and those built for minor gentlemen. And the latter buildings fall into a grey area which may overlap with some of the rural vernacular houses . Despite the potential overlap, the patterns of the two are so clearly defined that the risk of some distortion is worth taking. It was not deemed feasible to break these down further, since the numbers are small, and it includes public buildings, such as guildhalls, as well as houses.

The 'supra-vernacular' houses produce the same chronological profile as that indicated when buildings of all kinds are looked at together. While a handful of houses were erected throughout the thirteenth century, the numbers begin to increase in the last third, and show a marked rise in the early fourteenth. The lack of buildings during the rest of the troubled fourteenth century comes as no great surprise. But the dated buildings suggest that aristocratic and gentry building generally did not begin to pick up again until the middle of the fifteenth century. Moreover, it should be noted that eleven out of twenty - or 55% - of the examples in the period 1434-1466 are from Shropshire and Wales, with all but two of the rest coming from northern and midland counties such as Cumbria, Derbyshire, Lincolnshire and Nottinghamshire. As Richard Suggett has pointed out , the earliest gentry houses dated in Wales were only built in the 1430s, a conclusion which he claims can be applied to houses other than those which were tree-ring dated. At first sight this is surprising, given that close at hand in Shropshire gentry dwellings survive from the time of the early fourteenth-century peak which is apparent in other parts of England. He accounts for it by suggesting that earlier property was destroyed in Owain Glyndwr's revolt. This might explain the lack of fourteenth-century building in Wales, the start of the fifteenth-century boom in large houses may have been a wholly northern and western affair in England as well. In the south of England the tree-ring dates imply that the late medieval upsurge in building high status houses was deferred until the 1470s, and this is born out by other research. In Kent, very little high class building is known between the mid fourteenth and the late fifteenth century and in Hampshire there was a similar dearth and late fifteenth-century resurgence, which has been attributed to the introduction of demesne leasing on the great estates . One relevant point which might be made regarding the hiatus in gentry building relates to base crucks. If it is generally accepted that base crucks appear in houses built by those of superior status, then the fact that they die out in most areas after the 1330s is hardly surprising. By the time the gentry were building again, building styles in most regions had moved far beyond that stage.

A few buildings which may not be gentry houses survive from the thirteenth and early fourteenth centuries. Apart from a single example in Shropshire, they currently lie in southern England, primarily in Oxfordshire and Berkshire. There is no evidence for an early fourteenth-century peak, but clear signs of an increase in the last third of the century, continuing into the fifteenth. This is in marked contrast to the pattern of the known gentry houses, and seems to indicate a change in the circumstances of a number of peasants, perhaps at the expense of the landlords. In discussing this inference from the tree-ring dating of buildings, Christopher Dyer has related it to changes in prices and wages, and a renegotiation of the relationship between peasants and lords during and after the period of the Peasant's Revolt So far the dates show that the late fourteenth-century upsurge in vernacular building was largely confined to the south east, and that building in the rest of the south and the midlands followed only in the early to mid fifteenth-century. Surviving vernacular buildings in the north have only been dated in the second half of the century, and in Wales they apparently do not occur until well into the sixteenth. Wales apart, there is a massive increase in fifteenth-century rural houses, beginning in the middle years of the century, the tree-ring dating evidence suggesting that prosperity for a substantial number of peasants may have taken off that slight decline in dated buildings during the sixteenth century may simply be a reflection of work done, or it may be a general indication of the trend noted in Shropshire. It will be interesting to see what the national picture is like when a more truly representative sample has been obtained.

Since the numbers are fewer no attempt has been made to separate polite from vernacular, or even to distinguish houses from public buildings. When more urban examples have been sampled this should certainly be done, and at present aristocratic town houses, guildhalls and large inns form a high proportion of the dated buildings. No urban buildings have yet been dated before the last third of the thirteenth century, but when they appear they increase quickly, and are by no means all of high status. In Hampshire the earliest small houses so far dated are urban rather than rural, including one of 1292-3 and others of 1300, 1335 and 1340). Despite the small size of the sample, the numbers seem to increase significantly in the early fourteenth century, and in contrast to gentry building they continue to be built well into the middle of the century. Unlike rural buildings, there is far less disparity between north and south, and the urban buildings plotted from the first two thirds of the fourteenth century include examples from midland and northern towns such as Chester, Leicester, Ludlow, Nottingham, Shrewsbury and York.

In a manner similar to high status rural houses, there seems to be a falling off of urban building in the later fourteenth century, but the following two periods, from 1400 to the 1460s, have produced a substantial crop of dated examples. Thereafter, the numbers drop, and never recover. Regional variations in economy are likely to produce different patterns in different towns, and there are still too few examples spread over the whole country for any but the most cautious suggestions. However, these first results make one wonder whether tree-ring dating will not allow buildings to play a much more significant part than hitherto in arguments concerning urban prosperity and decline in the later Middle Ages . So far, and in marked contrast to the chronological spread of rural houses, the evidence suggests there was a great deal of urban building at all levels in the early fourteenth century, and again in the early fifteenth century, followed by a significant decline in the later fifteenth and early sixteenth centuries. As Christopher Dyer has remarked, buildings may have much to contribute to the study of urban-rural relationships which are currently concerning historians, and this first analysis of tree-ring dates bears out his suggestion . So far, few building recorders have engaged with this issue.

In terms of work likely to be undertaken from now on, the future looks bright. It is not just building recorders who see the value of tree-ring dating. More and more people are interested in using the technique for a variety of purposes. Not only national bodies, but regional and local authorities and organisations, are realising the potential of the technique in relation to the management and conservation of historic buildings. In the long run they will no doubt benefit by obtaining a more balanced view of the development of timber buildings in their counties sooner than that achieved in areas where research has sometimes had narrower aims.

In purely practical terms there are perhaps two main concerns. The first is that as the amount of work increases, so ought the number of professional dendrochronologists. Since several of the laboratories are located in universities it is to be hoped that plans for training new practitioners are in hand. The second problem is funding. At the time of writing the 'ball park' figure for dating a building or phase of building is £500 - £750. The main grant-giving bodies, such as the Leverhulme Foundation and the British Academy, have been generous in their support, and will no doubt continue to look favourably on suitable projects. Some of the large-scale projects without a single sponsor, for example those in Hampshire and Shropshire, have complicated and ingenious funding arrangements, mixing contributions from grant-giving bodies, local authorities, local societies, businesses and private individuals. Work on some of them depends largely on the professional dendrochronologists, who still have to solve outstanding problems relating to short ring sequences and the accuracy of estimation. Together with ecologists and building recorders, they need to continue to build chronologies in regions where these have proved difficult to establish, explore the dating of timber other than oak, research woodland management, and find answers to the task of dating buildings in awkward periods and parts of the country.

Other topics of research should be initiated by building recorders more directly. In the first place, projects already begun need to have their results written up and published for the benefit of everyone concerned. Secondly, those areas of the country where little has so far been attempted need to be explored, and those areas where only buildings of certain kinds or periods have been dated need to have the coverage extended, so that the resulting national sample is more truly representative. Thirdly, work should be done to test the reliability of older typologies and chronologies of building types and methods of construction, and the results analysed and published. Finally, it is conceivable that documentary historians have questions that buildings, once accurately dated, may be able to solve. Among these are questions relating to the pace of regional development, the changing fortunes of different social classes in the Middle Ages, the rise and decline of urban prosperity, and the differences in the development of town and country. Another area of research where tree-ring dating could play a significant part is in learning more of the organisation of the building trade itself. These are a few topics which are being, or could be, explored, and to them could be added many more by researchers whose perspectives are quite. Speculations of the kind ventured above, vulnerable to amendment though they are, have only become possible since the advent of tree-ring dating. The chronology rests on a different, potentially more accurate, basis from that used by Mercer. We no longer have to use terms such as 'late medieval', which cover a wide range of historical phases and experience, but can be far more specific. If we seek to use buildings as historical evidence, then getting the dating right is a pre-condition of fundamental importance.

5

THE PROCESS OF TREE GROWTH

INTRODUCTION

As we walk through the forest and view the trees, we remember they were once tiny seeds. Nearly all hardwood seeds are the same. They have an outer cover for protection, food and water inside to use for the first surge into growth, a part that has an affinity for water that will seek out the soil and become roots and a part with an affinity for light that will seek the sun and become leaves and branches. Nature gives all seeds another characteristic. An acorn will always grow into an oak tree and a pine seed will always grow into a pine tree.

While nature provides a seed all it needs to survive, she provides great opposition to survival. From the beginning, each seed must compete with its neighbor for water, food, sunlight and space in which to grow. Trees produce thousands of seeds. Very few grow to maturity. In fact, from a start of 10,000 seedlings per acre at age one year, the final stand of mature trees may number less than 50.

Seeds compete not only for food and sun with each other but many are eaten by forest animals, others are destroyed by insects and disease, and some simply do not find a suitable place to sprout.

Some trees produce flowers, from which the seeds come, before the leaves come out in the spring. These flowers produce seeds that ripen in the spring and fall to the ground and start to grow that year. Other seeds ripen and drop off in the fall and lay dormant over the winter and start to grow the following spring.

Temperature is the main factor in starting seed growth. When warm weather comes in the spring and the sun's rays hit the earth at a more direct angle, nature springs to life. Seeds have various means by which they are scattered over the countryside. An acorn falls down right under an oak tree but squirrels will often carry it away and bury it. Some seeds have wings that allow the wind to blow them over great distances. The outer covering of seeds can pass through a bird's digestive tract without damage, and be dropped far away. The maples, the yellow poplar and ash have winged seeds, the wild cherry is a seed spread by birds.

In order for any seed to sprout and develop it must have food, water, sunlight and warmth. Until it gets roots, a stem above ground, and some leaves or needles, the seed uses the food stored in its shell to develop growth. As roots go deeper into the soil they absorb water and minerals form the soil and send these up into the stem.

The leaves act as a chemical laboratory. In a process called photosynthesis, which takes place in the green leaves of a tree in the presence of chlorophyll and sunlight, the tree takes carbon dioxide from the air and manufactures starches and sugars and gives off oxygen as a waste product. The formula is simple but the process has never been artificially duplicated.

For each ton of wood that is produced, a little more than a ton of oxygen is released into the atmosphere. This takes place only on growing forests. In our old overmature forests where growth has become stagnate and decay has set in, more oxygen is used than produced. Thus, from an air quality standpoint alone it is essential to maintain healthy, viable forests in vigorous growing conditions.

In a process called transpiration, a tree gives off large quantities of water through a section of a leaf called stomata. All trees manufacture more food than they need for growing. The extra food is stored in the tree cells for use in the spring when it puts out leaves, flowers and seeds.

A tree grows upward from the tips of the branches, downward from the roots, and outward from the trunk. The roots anchor the tree to the ground, and the trunk gives support to the branches. As the tree grows from the food it manufacturers, it adds new layers of wood to its trunk. Because one is formed each year, these layers are called annual rings, and may be used to tell the age of the tree.

This is a drawing of the cross section of the stem of a tree. The outer bark is dead material, outside protection for the growing part of the tree. Next is the inner bark, composed if living cells through which water and food are conducted down into a tree, giving life to its roots and other parts. Next is the cambium layer, which you cannot see in a cross section without a magnifying glass. The cambium layer is made up of cells, those toward the outside make bark and those toward the inside make wood. Next is the sapwood, also composed mostly of living cells through which food and water are collected by the roots and sent up to the branches and leaves.

The centre of the stem is the heartwood. This is composed of dead cells that give the tree strength to stand. The heartwood was once sapwood but when new sapwood formed, the older died and formed the heartwood of the tree.

As you study the cross section of a tree, note that some annual rings are wider apart than others. When you see a wide space between the rings this means the tree grew faster at that time because it got more sunlight, water, and food. Lack of sunlight, food, water and competition with neighboring trees or being subjected to destructive forces such as forest fires, insects and disease, slow down the growth of the tree. The years marking slow growth show the rings closer together and narrow in width.

Many wood-using industries today are doing an excellent job of managing their forests and harvesting the trees so that other trees will grow and replace those which were removed. This practice, known as "sustainable forestry," assures that we will have trees of a variety of species and sizes growing forever to make the products we need in our daily lives.

PROTECTING TREES

The conflict between land development and tree protection seems to be a losing battle. Oftentimes, a building site has been chosen because of the presence of mature trees. These trees, however, have difficulty surviving the construction process. Although most developers would prefer to save trees on a property, they are often discouraged by past failures or regulations that force them to remove trees to locate utilities. Communication and cooperation among all participants involved in the building process (landowner, contractors, architect, landscape architect, arborist, etc.) is essential to ensure a successful tree-protection plan.

Once you have selected the trees to remain on the property, consider their location in deciding placement of the house, garage, driveway, walks and patio. Simply changing the angle of a building or curving a walk can preserve the essential root space of a prized tree. It is important at this point to be in close communication with your architect, who can help by locating buildings to harmonize with the natural terrain.

The key to the survival of trees in the years following construction is protection of the roots during construction. The three main causes of tree death during construction are soil compaction, grade changes and root severing.

SOIL COMPACTION

Soil compaction cuts off air and water to the tree roots. The damage caused by soil compaction occurs slowly, sometimes not becoming evident for several years. To prevent vehicular and foot traffic around the roots of protected trees, erect physical barriers beyond the dripline of individual trees, or better yet, groups of trees. When this is not possible, other protective methods can be used:

1. spreading several inches of wood chips in the root zone area;

2. bridging root areas with plates of steel. Work with the builder to locate and mark (with signs or flagging) all parking places for workers, construction roads, and areas for storage of building materials, soil and gravel.

RAISING THE EXISTING GRADE

Grade changes are often necessary during construction of a new building. When the grade around an established tree is being raised, consider methods of preventing injury to the tree before the fill is made rather than attempting to take corrective measures after the damage has been done. While the initial cost may be high, prevention is always cheaper and more effective than attempting to correct the situation after damage has been done.

Remove all vegetation, including underbrush and sod, beneath the branch spread of the tree. Break up the top 3 to 6 inches of soil carefully so as to disturb the least possible amount of roots. This allows better contact between the fill and soil surface. Apply fertilizer at recommended rates.

Construct an open-joint wall of shell, brick, rock or masonry in a circle around the tree trunk, with at least 1 to 2 feet between the wall and trunk. This wall should be as high as the top of the new grade. This opening is commonly referred to as a tree well.

Construct an aeration system using 4-inch agricultural clay tile or 4-inch perforated plastic pipe arranged in five to six horizontal lines radiating from the tree well like spokes in a wheel to a point beyond the branch spread. Allow excess moisture to drain away by installing the radial lines so they slope away from the trunk. Connect the outer ends of the radiating system with a circle of tile or perforated plastic pipe.

To provide vents, place 4- or 6-inch plastic pipe or bell tile upright over the junction of the radial lines with the circle. They should extend to the surface of the planned grade level. Extend the lower end of the aeration system to a curb or storm drain to carry excess moisture away from the root system.

Cover the exposed soil and tile system with rock or coarse gravel to a depth of 6 to18 inches, depending on the amount of fill. Follow this with a covering layer of gravel. Place a thin layer of straw, woven plastic or other porous material over the gravel to prevent soil from filtering into the gravel and stone. Fill with good topsoil to the desired grade.

To discourage rodents, fill the tree well with enough coarse gravel to cover the ends of the lines opening into the well. Also fill the upright bell tile and cover with a screen or grill.

The tree well can be left open, covered with a metal grill or wooden deck, or filled with a mixture of coarse sand and charcoal (50 percent each, by volume) to within several inches of the top. If filled with the sand/charcoal mixture, cover with pea gravel, decorative bark or other attractive material to allow air circulation through the tile system.

An alternate method can be used if 30 inches or less fill will be used. No tile or pipe is used – only gravel. Again, remove all sod and underbrush, break up the soil surface above the roots and apply fertilizer at recommended rates.

Starting at the dripline, apply from 3 to 6 inches of crushed stone or coarse gravel. Gradually increase the depth towards the trunk of the tree until it is 8 to 12 inches or deeper within 2 feet of the trunk. The gravel can reach the surface of the fill in the area extending 2 feet around the trunk of the tree. Cover the gravel with a thin layer of straw, woven plastic or other porous material to prevent soil from filtering into the gravel and sealing the air spaces. Spread good topsoil over the area to the desired depth. Use good, well-drained topsoil in making the fill in order to provide adequate aeration for normal root activity and tree growth.

LOWERING THE EXISTING GRADE

There will likely be less damage to a tree when the grade is lowered, unless a great amount of the root zone is exposed or removed. Removing 1 to 2 inches of soil normally will not affect the growth of a tree, especially if steps are taken to ensure that drought damage does not result from loss of roots. Use retaining walls or terraces to avoid excessive soil loss in the area of greatest root growth. When possible, spread mulch over the exposed area to help prevent soil erosion, reduce moisture loss and keep soil temperatures lower. Provide adequate water in the event of a prolonged drought.

Corrective Steps after a Fill is Made

If a fill has been in place long enough that the tree is already showing symptoms of deterioration, there is little that can be done to save the tree. If the fill was made recently, or if serious damage has not occurred, steps can be taken to correct the problem.

If the increase was greater than 12 inches, it will be necessary to install a tile and gravel aeration system as described above, excavating the soil to the original grade.

If the increase is less than 12 inches, remove the soil around the trunk, down to the original soil level, for a radius of 2 feet beyond the tree trunk. Install a dry well around the trunk to hold the fill soil in place. Drill or dig holes every 2 feet beneath the branch spread, starting about 2 feet from the well. Insert a 6-inch tile or plastic pipe and fill with coarse gravel to allow free air and gas exchange to the roots.

Severing Roots

Although some cutting of roots near construction is inevitable, much of it can be avoided with good planning and cooperation. It is not necessary to route underground utilities in a straight line from the street to the house. Careful route selection can often avoid the root systems of important trees. If this is not possible, reduce damage by tunneling beneath the roots. To reduce trenching for foundations, substitute posts and pillars for footers and walls.

Other Problems

Often when grade changes are made the terrain is altered, and there may be a change in how water drains from the land. If too much water drains into a wooded site, trees in that area may eventually die from lack of oxygen. It may be necessary to build a drainage system to maintain the previous amount of moisture that provided natural growing conditions for the existing trees. If sites are deprived of water, irrigation may be necessary to maintain existing trees.

Watch for equipment damage to limbs and trunks, and repair promptly. Chemicals and other products that are often dumped on a construction site can change the soil chemistry, weakening and oftentimes killing trees on the property. To prevent adverse effects on construction site soils:

- Spread heavy plastic tarp where concrete is to be mixed or sheet rock will be cut. These materials raise the pH, causing alkaline soils.
- Do not clean paintbrushes and tools over tree roots.
- Dispose of chemical wastes (paint thinner, oil, etc.) properly. Do not drain these wastes on site.

Annual or growth rings ~ in temperate climates there are two distinctive growth seasons, spring and summer ~ the spring growth is rapid and is shown as a broad band whereas the hotter, dryer summer growth shows up narrow. In tropical countries the growth rings are more even and difficult to distinguish.

k ~ the outer layer, corklike and provides protection to the tree from knocks and other damage.

Bast ~ the inner bark, carries enriched sap from the leaves to the cells where growth takes place.

Cambium ~ layer of living cells between the bast and the sapwood.

Crown ~ the branches and leaves that provides its typical summer shape.

Heartwood ~ mature timber, no longer carries sap, the heart of the tree, provides the strength of the tree. Usually a distinctive darker colour than the sapwood.

Medulla ray ~ (rays) food storage cells radiating from the medulla ~ provides a decorative feature found in quarter cut timber.

Pith or medulla ~ the centre of the tree, soft and pithy especially in the branches.

Sapwood ~ new growth, carries the raw sap up to the leaves. Usually lighter in colour than the heartwood, especially in softwoods.

Trunk ~ main structure of the tree, produces the commercial timber.

Root structure ~ Absorbs water and minerals from the soil. It is the anchor of the treee.

HARDWOODS AND SOFTWOODS

There are two main groups of timber producing trees used commercially; softwoods and hardwoods. These terms immediately create contention because they do not accurately describe the timber correctly.

Softwoods. Softwoods are coniferous trees and the timber is not necessarily 'soft'. They are 'evergreen'. (The *larch* is an exception) Their general characteristics are:

Straight, round but slender, tapering trunk.

The crown is narrow and rises to a point.

It has needle like or scale-like shaped leaves and it's fruit, i.e. it's seeds are carried in cones.

The bark is course and thick and softwoods are evergreen and as such do not shed their leaves in autumn.

Hardwoods. Hardwood trees are broadleaf and generally deciduous. Their timber is not necessarily hard. For instance, balsa (the timber used for making model planes) is a hardwood. The general characteristics are:

- Stout base that scarcely tapers but divides into branches to form a wide, round crown.
- The leaves are broad and may have single or multi lobes.
- The bark may be smooth or course and varies in thickness and colours.
- Its fruit may be: nuts, winged fruits, pods, berries, or fleshy fruits.

MAINTENANCE OF THE PLANTATION

Once a plantation has been established, the work should not be considered finished. It will be necessary, for example, to protect the plantation against weather, fire, insects and fungi, and animals. A variety of cultural treatments also may be required to meet the purpose of the plantation.

Weather Phenomena

The occurrence of damaging weather phenomena is usually unpredictable. Little can be done to protect forest plantations against the damage caused by weather, except to grow tree and shrub species known to be resistant to the detrimental effects of local weather patterns, or locating the stands of trees or shrubs in sheltered areas. Some tree and shrub species are more windfirm than others, or are less prone to crowns and branches breaking off in high winds. Other species are more tolerant to salt spray and, therefore, can be used for planting in belts along exposed seaward flanks to give protection to other less tolerant species forming the main plantation. Thin-barked species are more susceptible to damage and to subsequent attacks by insects or fungi than are other species.

Fire

Fire damage by fire imposes a serious threat to plantations. The fire risk is generally high in the dryer climatic regions; but, even in relatively moist or high rainfall areas, there may be warm and dry spells when the fire risk is high. Fire risk should be a major consideration from the early stages of plantation development.

Fires can originate from natural causes, such as lightning, but many occur as a result of the activities of man. Plantation fires can start from fires spreading from farmland on the perimeter, from the activities of hunters, or from burning by herdsman to improve livestock grazing. There have been instances of deliberate burning to create employment (in the fire suppression and subsequent replanting) or to show disapproval of forest policies. It is not possible to prevent a climatic build-up of fire hazard conditions, but much can be done to minimize the risk of fire through public education and involving local people in forestry.

A main principle in protecting forest plantations against fire is that, where there is insufficient combustible material to allow a ground fire to develop, there is little or no fire risk. Dangerous and damaging plantation fires can only develop when fire is able to occur at ground level.

In many parts of the world, annual or periodic burning of vegetation is commonly practiced to improve grazing conditions, to reduce the build-up of fuels, or to improve soil fertility through accumulation of ash.

Insects and Fungi

Most insects and fungi are selective of the host species. In their natural environment, trees and shrubs normally attain a state of equilibrium with indigenous pests. However, when exotic trees and shrubs are planted, exotic pests can also be introduced. Quite often, these exotic pests readily adapt themselves to the conditions of their new habitat. In general, the risk of damage from pests is higher when the plants are physiologically weakened from planting on unsuitable sites, improper site preparation, inefficient planting, adverse climatic conditions, or neglect of weeding and other maintenance operations. But even healthy trees and shrubs are attacked at times. For many insects and fungi, no control measures are available; when this is the case, the best precaution is to plant tree and shrub species or varieties known to be resistant to the pests.

The main precautions to be taken in guarding against possible future damage from insects and fungi are to plant tree or shrub species that are suitable to the climatic and soil conditions of the site, and to make surveys of indigenous pests to ensure that none are among the known forms to which the selected species is susceptible; but this is seldom easy, especially in view of the gaps in available knowledge on site requirements and susceptibility of exotic species to insects and fungi. To obtain this needed information, carefully controlled experiments should be initiated before developing large-scale planting programmes.

Care taken in establishment and maintenance operations during the early years of a plantation (resulting in healthy vigorous young trees or shrubs) can help to make a plantation more resistant to insects and fungi. However, when evidence of pest attack appears, it should be investigated promptly and the cause identified. Various control measures are available; these may be silvicultural, chemical, biological, or mechanical.

Silvicultural measures include well timed, careful thinnings after establishment of the forest plantation. Through thinning, poor and suppressed stems are eliminated, maintaining the plantation in a thrifty and vigorous growing condition. In young plantations, prompt removal and destruction of infested trees and shrubs can be effective in preventing the spread of the pest attacks to the rest of the plantation. Where a threat of infection is known to exist, planting of tree or shrub mixed species also can be considered a silvicultural control measure.

One disadvantage of mixed plantings is that subsequent forest management can be complicated; however, this may be avoided, at least partially, by planting alternate blocks or wide belts with different tree or shrub species, forming barriers to the spread of a pest or disease from the initial point of infection.

Insects and fungi can often be checked by applications of appropriate chemical insecticides or fungicides. Usually, these chemicals are available as liquids (or wettable powder), dusts, or smokes. Spraying with hand-operated spray guns or portable mist-blowers is frequently used to control attacks in young plantations; with canopy closure, aerial spraying and dusting or smoking can be more effective and cheaper. Only previously tested and environmentally sound insecticides and fungicides should be prescribed for use.

Biological control of insects has been employed with success in some situations; in most instances, the introduction of a parasite to control the insects is required. The greatest success in biological control is usually achieved after the problem has grown to epidemic proportions.

Mechanical control, either by physically removing and destroying the pests or by eliminating the alternative hosts, can be effective.

Wild Animals

Wild animals damage to forest plantations by wild animals mainly takes the form of tree browsing or de-barking. In general, there are three orders of wild animals responsible for damage: rodents (rats, mice, and moles and squirrels); lagomophs (hares and rabbits); and artiodactyls (deer, antelopes, pigs and buffaloes). The principal methods of controlling damage by wild animals involves the use of fences, hedges or ditches, trapping and removal, and poison baits.

Domestic Animals

In some countries, grazing or browsing by sheep, goats and cattle can be a menace to young plantations. At times, hedges and fences are used to prevent intrusion by domestic animals. Where fencing costs are high, trespass by livestock can be controlled by guards.

In many dry areas, grazing by goats is a traditional land use. Extensive enclosures of forest plantations can impose drastic changes in the habits and economies of the rural communities affected. In such situations, it would be unwise to initiate planting programmes unless alternative means of livelihood can be provided beforehand; generally, this requires the integration of community development schemes (for example, improved agriculture or animal husbandry, better communications, schools, or medical welfare) and increased opportunities for employment by the development of rural industries (such as afforestation programmes and rural forest industries).

CULTURAL TREATMENTS

Cultural operations are required to promote the conditions that are favorable to the survival and subsequent growth and yield of the trees or shrubs in the plantation. In most forest plantations, cultural operations are concerned with preventing the trees and shrubs from being suppressed by competing vegetation; quite often, this treatment is called weeding. Other cultural treatments are thinning to achieve a desired spacing among the trees or shrubs, and the periodic watering of the plants.

Weeding

Weeding is a cultural operation that eliminates or suppresses undesirable vegetation which, if no action were taken, would impair the growth of the plantation crop. This undesirable vegetation competes with trees and shrubs for light, water, and nutrients; weeding increases the availability of all or the most critical of these elements to the trees and shrubs. A primary objective of weeding is to promote growth and development of the plantation crop, while keeping the costs of the operation within acceptable limits.

A main factor affecting the intensity and duration of weeding treatments is the relationship between the tree or shrub crop and the weeds. On some sites, the plantation crop eventually grows through the weeds, dominates the site, and becomes established; on such sites, the function of weeding is to increase crop uniformity and speed up the process of establishment and growth. On other sites, the type or density of the weed growth is such that, in the early stage of a forest plantation, it may suppress and kill some or all of the planted trees or shrubs; in such areas, the main purpose of weeding is to reduce mortality and maintain an adequate stocking of trees or shrubs.

The methods of weeding involve either suppression or elimination of the competing vegetation. Suppression of weeds consists of physically beating down or crushing them, or cutting the weeds back at or above ground level. Weed elimination can be achieved by killing the weeds, destroying the whole plant either by cultivation or by the use of chemicals. Weeding may be total or partial.

Thinning

Thinning of forest plantations, particularly those established for wood production, may be required to obtain the desired spacing between the trees. In general, this spacing is a compromise between a "wide" spacing to reduce planting costs and inter-tree competition in times of drought, and a "close" spacing to attain early canopy closure, the suppression of weeds, the reduction of weeding costs, and natural pruning of branches through shading.

In "first-rotation" forest plantations, the thinning objective is frequently to adjust the initial spacing among plants, so that the size and type of tree or shrub required is attained on a short rotation, without secondary thinning treatments. Where a tree or shrub of larger size and higher quality is required, closer than final spacing is often prescribed in an initial thinning; usually, some form of secondary thinning is necessary as a subsequent treatment. The element of selection in thinning should ensure that the increment growth of the final crop is concentrated on the best stems.

Regardless of the purpose of the thinning operation, it should follow closely the timing and spacing requirements that are outlined in a prescribed thinning schedule for the area.

Watering

Watering often, forest plantations in arid regions need at least periodic watering during the first growing season to obtain a satisfactory survival rate. Watering should begin after the cessation of rains, when the moisture content of the soil has fallen to near the wilting coefficient; then watering should be repeated at intervals until the onset of the next rainy season. Before each watering, the area around the tree should be cleared of weeds, and a shallow basin should be made around the stem of each tree or shrub to collect as much water as possible.

Watering can be an expensive operation, especially on terrain too steep or too rough for the passage of tank vehicles. Pack animals may be required to carry drums of water to the plantation site. Watering can be uneconomic for large forest plantations, particularly when the source of water is a long distance from the plantation, but it may be justified in the case of small plantations or for establishing roadside avenues.

In some instances, regular cultivation and weeding, especially during the first growing season, are sufficient measures to conserve soil moisture for satisfactory survival of the plants, eliminating the need for watering.

HARVESTING OPERATIONS

For forest plantations that are established for purposes of wood production, trees and shrubs are harvested once they attain the "optimum size" for the wood product wanted. From a biological standpoint, trees and shrubs should not be cut until they have at least grown to the minimum size required for production utilization. Beyond attaining the minimum size, the question of when to harvest must still be answered, however.

Quite often, the average annual growth rates of a forest plantation can be used as a guide in determining when to harvest wood. In general, the average annual growth of trees and shrubs increases slowly during the initial years of plantation establishment, reaches a maximum, and then falls more gradually. Trees and shrubs usually should not be allowed to grow beyond the point of maximum average annual growth, which is the age of maximum productivity; foresters call this the "rotation" age of the forest plantation.

To determine the average annual growth rate of a forest plantation at a point-in-time, the volume and age of the trees or shrubs must be estimated; then the average annual growth (at the specified point-in-time) is determined by dividing the standing volume by the corresponding age. Again, careful measurements of volumes and known ages are necessary for this determination.

Economic considerations also help to determine when to harvest trees and shrubs for wood products. When based solely on market factors, the time to harvest is when the profit is maximized. Profit is maximized when the returns generated from harvesting and selling the wood minus the costs of harvesting and (when required) processing the wood into the desired products is the greatest.

The methods of felling trees and shrubs, cutting the stems and branchwood into the desired lengths, and removing the wood from the plantation site should be chosen to minimize degradation of the site. Axes, saws, wedges and sledges may be all that are necessary to fell the trees and shrubs and cut them into the desired lengths. Power-chainsaws are used in many instances; while their use makes harvesting easier, their high cost of operation can make then uneconomical.

Once the trees and shrubs are felled and cut into desired lengths, they must be carried or pulled to loading points for transport to processing sites or directly to a market place. When stem lengths are too heavy to carry, a simple drag or sled can be employed to move them, using an available power source, such as a domestic animal or a tractor. When residual trees or shrubs are left in the forest plantation, the harvesting operation should be carried out to prevent damage to this standing resource.

It is important that the methods of harvesting should be selected to "match" the skills of the people who will harvest the trees or shrubs. Once again, advanced planning will be necessary to ensure that the labour and required equipment will be available for use at the needed time.

HIGHLIGHTS OF SECTION

In selecting appropriate tree and shrub species for plantations in arid zones, site condition information (on climate, soils, topography, biotic factors, vegetation, and water table levels), as well as knowledge of socio-economic factors, must be known. Once the site and species have been selected for planting, fencing which marks boundaries and protects the trees and shrubs should be erected, if required. For a successful tree or shrub crop, site preparation is often necessary; site preparation may include removal of competing vegetation, enhancing water catchment, reducing water runoff, providing good soil conditions, eliminating fire hazards, and preparing the soil.

In general, planting coincides with the rainy season. After planting, use of opaque plastic films can impede evaporation and inhibit weed growth around potted stock. The spacings of the plantings should be wide enough to prevent competition for soil moisture, or when part of management, to accommodate machinery used for irrigation.

Maintenance of forest plantations includes protecting the plants from detrimental climatic conditions, fire, insects and fungi, and animals. Maintenance may include measures that are silvicultural (such as well-timed and careful removal of damaged trees and shrubs), chemical (with insecticides or fungicides), biological (with parasites), or mechanical (removing or destroying pests, erecting fences, etc.). Because trespass by man can threaten the success of a planting programme, planning should also include methods of dealing with this potential problem.

Cultural treatments to promote favorable growth conditions include weeding, thinning, and watering. Harvesting operations, when required, should match the skills of the people who will perform the tasks.

6

AGE OF A TREE

INTRODUCTION

As trees age, they get bigger. With increased size comes increased surface area for other plants to colonize, more gnarled and fissured bark, rot-holes and caverns in the trunk, together with the production of flowers, fruits and seeds. Past a certain size, the tree will begin to senesce and bits of it will die off, remaining attached to provide standing rotting wood microhabitats. Old trees therefore develop a wealth of microhabitats for other organisms and a large surface area for colonization. By extension, the more old trees a particular woodland contains, the greater its biodiversity is likely to be.

In general, biodiversity within woodlands increases both with the age of the individual trees which it contains and the historical age of the wood.

It seems too obvious to even comment upon, but as trees age, they get bigger! A small sapling, only a few metres tall, with relatively smooth bark and few branches, will gradually acquire, along with added height, a complicated branching pattern and myriads of individual branches and twigs.

Each year that the tree grows, a new ring of wood (xylem) is laid down within the trunk and each of the branches. This provides the conduit which will carry water to all parts of the tree. As a result, with each successive new layer of wood, the tree's girth increases. The outer layer of bark must therefore also expand to accommodate the new girth and new layers of bark will be laid down. Bark acts in a similar way to our skin, protecting against attack by fungi, bacteria, insects and other animals. It is also water-proof and protects underlying layers from drying out.

The type of bark varies depending on the species of tree. Some trees have a very thin bark, which remains relatively smooth, while others have a very thick bark. In some trees, the older bark readily peels away or breaks off. In this case the bark tends to be very papery. In species where the older layers of bark remain attached, a very thick layer can build up on the outside of the tree which is only gradually worn away.

As the tree matures, it will also begin to flower and set seed. An Oak tree, for example, will not be mature enough to flower for approximately 50 years. At this point the tree begins to offer a host of new opportunities for other life, with seasonal feasts of flowers and highly nutritious fruits or seeds on offer.

The increase in the number of branches and twigs as the tree grows, allows for the space to produce a much greater number of leaves. The more leaves the tree has functioning, the more food it can produce for itself through the process of photosynthesis. However, there is a trade-off here. The more branches the tree has, the more wood must be laid down at the start of each year in order to supply the leaves with the raw materials necessary for the process.

Our tree is now Old! If it is an Oak, it may by now have presided over several hundred years of local history. It has a hugely increased surface area over its sapling days. It may be tens of metres tall. It has an amazingly complex series of branches, each with its own smaller branches and twigs. All of this enormous surface area provides a substrate for other life to colonize, from algae, mosses, ferns and lichens, to climbing plants such ivy. These plants offer a wealth of microhabitats in their own right. Many of them are very slow-growing and may require up to hundreds of years to develop a significant presence.

Periodically, the tree will also flower and set seed, providing seasonal abundance for many different animals. The enormous number of leaves produced are fodder for a staggering number of individual invertebrates from aphids and leaf miners, to caterpillars. When the leaves die and fall, they will slowly rot away on the woodland floor, providing yet another microhabitat for woodland life. The older the tree, the more leaves are produced and so the more of this resource that is available.

Old, dead branches, still attached, will slowly rot away, providing food for the many species inhabiting standing dead wood. The heart wood may begin to rot away, opening up holes and caverns within the trunk, which can be occupied by many opportunistic creatures. Knot holes may have developed higher up, providing nesting sites and rain water traps. These will often develop their own very characteristic fauna, capable of completing their life cycle in the short life span of this lofty temporary pool.

The value of ancient trees for biodiversity is now well recognised. Interest in ancient trees in Britain, as well as databases, are being developed through such initiatives as the Ancient Tree Forum, the Veteran Trees Initiative and through implementation of UK Biodiversity Action Plans for such habitats as Wood-pasture and Parkland.

Because of the individual biodiversity value of ancient trees, the more old trees a woodland contains, the greater its overall biodiversity is likely to be. In addition to this, the length of time an area has been continuously wooded is also relevant. Thus ancient woodlands will often contain species which are peculiar to them and which are rarely found in newer woodlands. Many of these species are slow to colonize new habitats, as well as slow-growing. Newly planted woods will predominantly contain those species which are quick colonizers, or which have survived in the seed-bed from previous land use.

PINE

Pines are coniferous trees in the genus *Pinus,* in the family Pinaceae. They make up the monotypic subfamily Pinoideae.

There are about 115 species of pine, although different authorities accept between 105 and 125 species.

Pines are native to most of the Northern Hemisphere. In Eurasia, they range from the Canary Islands and Scotland east to the Russian Far East, and the Philippines, north to just over 70°N in Norway (Scots Pine) and eastern Siberia (Siberian Dwarf Pine), and south to northernmost Africa, the Himalaya and Southeast Asia, with one species (Sumatran Pine) just crossing the Equator in Sumatra to 2°S. In North America, they range from 66°N in Canada (Jack Pine) south to 12°N in Nicaragua (Caribbean Pine). The highest diversity in the genus occurs in Mexico and California.

Pines have been introduced in subtropical and temperate portions of the Southern Hemisphere, including Chile, Brazil, South Africa, Australia, and New Zealand, where they are grown widely as a source of timber, and some species are becoming invasive.

MORPHOLOGY

Pines are evergreen and resinous trees (rarely shrubs) growing to 3–80 m tall, with the majority of species reaching between 15-45 m tall. The smallest are Siberian Dwarf Pine and Potosi Pinyon, and the tallest, Sugar Pine. Pines are long-lived, typically reaching ages of 100–1,000 years, some even more. The longest-lived is the Great Basin Bristlecone Pine *Pinus longaeva*, one individual of which at 4840 years old in 2008 is one of the oldest living organisms in the world.

The bark of most pines is thick and scaly, but some species have thin, flaking bark. The branches are produced in regular "pseudo whorls", actually a very tight spiral but appearing like a ring of branches arising from the same point. Many pines are *uninodal*, producing just one such whorl of branches each year, from buds at the tip of the year's new shoot, but others are *multinodal*, producing two or more whorls of branches per year. The spiral growth of branches, needles and cone scales are arranged in Fibonacci number ratios. The new spring shoots are sometimes called "candles"; they are covered in brown or whitish bud scales and point upward at first, then later turn green and spread outward. These "candles" offer foresters a means to evaluate fertility of the soil and vigour of the trees.

Foliage

Pines have four types of leaves:

1. *Seed leaves* (cotyledons) on seedlings, borne in a whorl of 4-24.
2. *Juvenile leaves*, which follow immediately on seedlings and young plants, 2-6 cm long, single, green or often blue-green, and arranged spirally on the shoot. These are produced for six months to five years, rarely longer (and also produced later in life after injury in some pines).
3. *Scale leaves*, similar to bud scales, small, brown and non-photosynthetic, and arranged spirally like the juvenile leaves.
4. *Needles*, the adult leaves, which are green (photosynthetic), bundled in clusters (*fascicles*) of (1-) 2-5 (-6) needles together, each fascicle produced from a small bud on a dwarf shoot in the axil of a scale leaf. These bud scales often remain on the fascicle as a basal sheath. The needles persist for 1.5-40 years, depending on species. If a shoot is damaged (e.g. eaten by an animal), the needle fascicles just below the damage will generate a bud which can then replace the lost leaves.

A fully mature Monterey Pine cone on the forest floor.

Pines are mostly monoecious, having the male and female cones on the same tree, though a few species are sub-dioecious with individuals predominantly, but not wholly, single-sex. The male cones are small, typically 1-5 cm long, and only present for a short period (usually in spring, though autumn in a few pines), falling as soon as they have shed their pollen. The female cones take 1.5-3 years (depending on species) to mature after pollination, with actual fertilization delayed one year. At maturity the female cones are 3-60 cm long. Each cone has numerous spirally arranged scales, with two seeds on each fertile scale; the scales at the base and tip of the cone are small and sterile, without seeds. The seeds are mostly small and winged, and are anemophilous (wind-dispersed), but some are larger and have only a vestigial wing, and are bird-dispersed. At maturity, the cones usually open to release the seeds. but in some of the bird-dispersed species (e.g. Whitebark Pine), the seeds are only released by the bird breaking the cones open. In others, the *fire climax pines* (e.g. Monterey Pine, Pond Pine), the seeds are stored in closed ("serotinous") cones for many years until a forest fire kills the parent tree; the cones are also opened by the heat and the stored seeds are then released in huge numbers to re-populate the burnt ground.

CLASSIFICATION

Pines are divided into three subgenera, based on cone, seed and leaf characters:

- Subgenus: *Strobus* (white or soft pines). Cone scale without a sealing band. Umbo terminal. Seedwings adnate. One fibrovascular bundle per leaf.
- Subgenus: *Ducampopinus* (pinyon, lacebark and bristlecone pines). Cone scale without a sealing band. Umbo dorsal. Seedwings articulate. One fibrovascular bundle per leaf.
- Subgenus: *Pinus* (yellow or hard pines). Cone scale with a sealing band. Umbo dorsal. Seedwings articulate. Two fibrovascular bundles per leaf.

ECOLOGY

Pines grow well in acid soils, some also on calcareous soils; most require good soil drainage, preferring sandy soils, but a few, e.g. Lodgepole Pine, will tolerate poorly drained wet soils. A few are able to sprout after forest fires, e.g. Canary Island Pine. Some species of pines, e.g. Bishop Pine, need fire to regenerate and their populations slowly decline under fire suppression regimes. Several species are adapted to extreme conditions imposed by elevation and latitude; see e.g. Siberian Dwarf Pine, Mountain Pine, Whitebark Pine and the bristlecone pines. The pinyon pines and a number of others, notably Turkish Pine, are particularly well adapted to growth in hot, dry semi-desert climates.

The seeds are commonly eaten by birds and squirrels. Some birds, notably the Spotted Nutcracker, Clark's Nutcracker and Pinyon Jay, are of importance in distributing pine seeds to new areas. Pine needles are sometimes eaten by some Lepidoptera (butterfly and moth) species (see list of Lepidoptera that feed on pines) and also the Symphytan species Pine Sawfly.

USES

Pines are among the most commercially important of tree species, valued for their timber and wood pulp throughout the world. In temperate and tropical regions, they are fast-growing softwoods that will grow in relatively dense stands, their acidic decaying needles inhibiting the sprouting of competing hardwoods. Commercial pines are grown in plantations for timber that is denser, more resinous, and therefore more durable than spruce (*Picea*). Pine wood is widely used in high-value carpentry items such as furniture, window frames, paneling and floors.

Many pine species make attractive ornamental plantings for parks and larger gardens, with a variety of dwarf cultivars being suitable for smaller spaces. Pines are also commercially grown and harvested for Christmas trees. Pine cones, the largest and most durable of all conifer cones are craft favorites. Pines boughs, always appreciated, especially in wintertime for their pleasant smell and greenery, are popularly cut for decorations.

Pine needles serve as food for various Lepidoptera. See List of Lepidoptera which feed on Pines.

Food Uses

The soft, moist, white inner bark (cambium) found clinging to the woody outer bark is edible and very high in vitamins A and C. It can be eaten raw in slices as a snack or dried and ground up into a powder for use as a thickener in stews, soups, and other foods, such as pine bread. A tea made by steeping young, green pine needles in boiling water (known as "tallstrunt" in Sweden) is high in vitamins A and C.

Etymology

The modern English name *pine* derives from Latin *Pinus* by way of French *pin*; similar names are used in other Romance languages. In the past (pre-19th century) they were often known as *fir*, from Old Norse *fyrre*, by way of Middle English *firre*. The Old Norse name is still used for pines in some modern north European languages, in Danish, *fyr*, in Norwegian and Swedish, *furu*, and *Föhre* in German, but in modern English, "fir" is now restricted to Fir (*Abies*) and *Douglas-fir* (Pseudotsuga).

Taxonomic Notes

Some authors segregate the yews and plum-yews (Taxaceae and Cephalotaxaceae) as Order Taxales, and there is general agreement that they warrant distinction above the rank of family. Some authors segregate the family Cupressaceae into two families, Cupressaceae and Taxodiaceae; see Cupressaceae for relevant remarks. Reveal (1998) proposes that most of the conifer families be elevated to the rank of Order. However, he further retains all families as treated here, with one exception: the genus *Phyllocladus*, here assigned to the Podocarpaceae, is raised to the rank of Family within Order Podocarpales Pulle ex Reveal 1992.

Description

Conifers usually have needle-shaped or scalelike leaves, and nearly all are evergreen. They typically have straight trunks with horizontal branches varying more or less regularly in length from bottom to top, so that the trees are conical in outline. They are characterized by having staminate or pollen-producing cones; most also bear ovulate or seed-producing cones.

Cosmopolitan, excepting polar regions, the highest mountains, the driest deserts, and a few oceanic islands. Species in the Pinaceae are almost entirely confined to the northern hemisphere, while the Podocarpaceae and Araucariaceae are most widespread in the southern hemisphere and tropical northern latitudes. The Taxaceae are very widespread, although nowhere abundant, in the northern hemisphere and a bit of the southern. Cephalotaxaceae are confined to Asia, and *Sciadopitys* is only native in Japan. Some of the most widespread tree species in the world are found in the northern forests, where a handful of *Larix, Picea* and *Pinus* species circle the globe across Scandinavia, Russia, Alaska and Canada.

The largest of all is *Sequoiadendron giganteum*, in the Cupressaceae. A hundred years or so ago the largest was probably *Sequoia sempervirens*, also in the Cupressaceae, but the finest stands in that species were all destroyed by the loggers long ago; only remnants remain. The third largest is *Agathis australis*, in the Araucariaceae. Here again the finest forests were taken by the loggers, and we can only speculate on how large some of the vanished giants were; they may have rivaled *Sequoia* and *Sequoiadendron*. *Pseudotsuga menziesii* representing the Pinaceae, *Podocarpus totara* representing the Pinaceae, and *Taxus sumatrana* representing the Taxaceae are all distinctly impressive trees. Little *Cephalotaxus harringtonia* representing the Cephalotaxaceae and *Sciadopitys verticillata* representing the Sciadopityaceae, on the other hand, seldom attract much attention.

The Great Basin bristlecone pine, *Pinus longaeva*, can live nearly 5,000 years and is the undisputed champion. It is often described as the oldest living thing. Ages of over 3,000 years have been shown for *Fitzroya cupressoides* and *Sequoiadendron giganteum*, both in the Cupressaceae, and there are probably more really ancient trees in the Cupressaceae than in any other family. Next up is the Podocarpaceae; the Huon pine, *Lagarostrobos franklinii*, can live for 2,500 years. None of the other families have species that have been proven to live over 1,000 years, but such ages are probably achieved by *Taxus baccata* in the Taxaceae, and by *Agathis australis* and *Araucaria araucana* in the Araucariaceae. I should mention that *Taxus baccata* could reasonably be expected to live a very, very long time - thousands of years - but it lives by growing at the cambium while dying at the heart, so that a tree might grow in one place for a thousand years and yet not have any wood in it more than a few hundred years old. Does this make the tree a thousand years old?

A great many species have received attention, and in fact, unless someone has done some work with ginkgo , conifers are the only gymnosperms that have received attention from dendrochronologists.

Conifers are one of the world's most important renewable resources. Most economic and cultural exploitation concerns members of the families Pinaceae and Cupressaceae, with Araucariaceae (in Australia and South America) and Podocarpaceae (in scattered tropical locales) locally important. See genus and species descriptions for particulars.

Several conifers, particularly in the genera *Agathis* (Araucariaceae), *Abies*, and *Pinus* (Pinaceae), produce economically important resins. Resins are sticky, liquid, organic substances that usually harden when exposed to air into brittle, amorphous, solid substances. Natural resins are classified according to their physical and chemical properties into hard resins, oleoresins, and gum resins (Moussouris and Regato 1999).

Conifers have a long and complex spiritual tradition in our culture. Their evergreen nature has made them symbols of immortality; *Taxus baccata* is a good example. Spiritual powers were also attributed to the cedar of Lebanon, *Cedrus libani*. Other trees were so important to the lives of aboriginal peoples that they were personified or worshipped; examples include the western redcedar, *Thuja plicata*; the Bunya pine, *Araucaria bidwillii*; and the kauri, *Agathis australis*. Even in our modern secular culture, people still speak reverently about species such as the Coast redwood (*Sequoia sempervirens*) and the *Sequoiadendron*.

Conifers are very popular ornamentals, widely used in landscaping. Good places to observe the diversity of conifers include arboreta, botanical gardens, zoos, and often city parks. However, I feel they are best seen in the wild, growing and reproducing in their native habitat. The species pages on this site will give you information helpful in finding such sites.

FERTILIZING TREES

Fertilizer applications are used during the growing season to improve the health and appearance of trees. Most deciduous trees should be fertilized once every two to three years. Evergreens may be fertilized in the spring, but less often than deciduous trees.

Since trees have their greatest need for nutrients in the spring, fertilizer should be applied any time between leaf drop in the fall and leafing out in the spring. The health and vigor of a tree may be improved by fertilizers up to July 1. Beyond that time, new growth stimulated by the fertilizer may not have sufficient time to harden off before winter.

- Trees growing in naturalized areas where little or no mowing takes place and leaves are not collected usually will not need regular fertilizing.

- Homeowners have two main methods of applying fertilizer to trees. The fertilizer can be applied directly to the soil surface or it can be applied below the soil surface via augured holes.
- Spreading the fertilizer on the soil surface is the easiest and least expensive method.
- Putting fertilizer below the soil surface is more difficult but gets phosphorus and potassium into the root zone and provides the additional benefit of aeration. This can be accomplished by using a root feeder or drilling holes in the soil.
- Using a hose-attached root feeder will get the material into the root zone in liquid form. Water flows past premeasured tablets in an enclosed chamber and passes through a hollow needle inserted into the soil about 8 to 12 inches deep. Follow label directions to get the calculated amount of material equally distributed to each of the insertion sites.

Another method of application is to make holes approximately 2 to 3 feet apart at and beyond the drip line of the tree. Holes are drilled into the soil with a power auger 8 to 12 inches deep, slanting toward the center of the tree. The calculated amount of fertilizer for the tree then is distributed equally to the available holes, followed by a thorough watering to put the fertilizer into solution. Trees that are showing symptoms of iron chlorosis will benefit best from this method of application.

Foliar feeding of small trees is becoming more popular with homeowners. This form of fertilization is used to correct deficiencies of micronutrients such as iron or manganese. These deficiencies typically show up in soil with high pH values. Since neither of these elements stimulate excessive growth, but they do correct a chlorotic (intervienal leaf yellowing) condition, they can be applied anytime during the growing season. See Table 1 for trees tolerant to high soil pH.

Foliar spray also is used to help get young trees established in the landscape and help recently transplanted trees overcome the shock of being moved. As with other methods, be sure to follow label directions to avoid excessive fertilizer salt damage.

The tendency of novice homeowners is to overfertilize because estimating the amount needed in such a small volume of soil is difficult. To be safe, use slow-release and/or natural organic fertilizers mixed with the backfill soil. (see sketch: "Proper Planting and Fertilizing New Trees").

The amount of fertilizer usually is determined by the nitrogen (N) content of the material. For example, a standard recommendation is 1 pound of actual nitrogen per 1,000 square feet. This can be calculated easily by taking an example of 20-5-10 fertilizer. Multiply the weight of the fertilizer, in this case 50 pounds, by 20 percent, the amount of nitrogen (50 x 20% =10 pounds). With this knowledge, we take the amount desired, 1 pound of N, and divide it by 20 percent (1/20% = 5 pounds of 20-5-10 fertilizer needed to provide 1 pound of nitrogen to 1,000 square feet). This bag of fertilizer with this analysis of nitrogen would be able to treat a total of 10,000 square feet of area at the rate of 1 pound of actual nitrogen per 1,000 square feet (10 pounds of nitrogen in 50 pounds of fertilizer @ 1 lb/1,000 sf = 10,000 sf).

When looking at a bag of fertilizer for nutrient information, the data will note that nitrogen is available from different sources – synthetic organic, natural organic (expressed as WIN – water-insoluble nitrogen) or inorganic (expressed as WSN – water-soluble nitrogen). When selecting a fertilizer, one-third to one-half of the nitrogen source should be in one of the organic or WIN forms. Nitrogen in this form is available more slowly and is not as apt to leach through the soil as quickly as the WSN forms might. Typical slow release forms of nitrogen are urea formaldehyde (UF), isobutylidene diurea (IBDU), methylene ureas (MU) and sulfur-coated urea (SCU).

The fertilizer/herbicide products available on the homeowner market for turf areas are a potential source for damage to trees when applied to areas under the tree canopy. The active component is often Dicamba, which may cause decline and stress, and possibly contribute to the loss of established trees.

APPLICATION CALCULATIONS

The area to be fertilized under a tree canopy forms a circle. To calculate the square footage, take the radius squared x 3.14.

Suppose a tree has a canopy radius of 15 feet. This would equal 706 square feet that would be considered for fertilizer application. The 50-pound bag of fertilizer that is going to be used has a nitrogen analysis of 20 percent. To get 1 pound of actual nitrogen per 1,000 square feet over that area of 706 square feet, we divide the area to be fertilized by 1,000 (706/1,000 = 0.706), which means about 0.7pound of this fertilizer should be applied.

Another method of fertilizer calculation is to measure the trunk diameter of the tree at about 4.5 feet above ground level. Using this method, the amount to use is 1 pound of fertilizer for each inch of trunk diameter, if the analysis is 20-5-10 or something similar. If the analysis for nitrogen is 10 percent or lower, then use 2 pounds per inch of diameter. Excessive nitrogen application should be avoided, especially on young trees, because this may cause soft, spindly growth.

Whether using the broadcast, root feeder or soil auger method of application, spread the nutrients as uniformly and evenly as possible for uniform nutrient uptake. Most of the fibrous roots are near or beyond the drip line of the tree and absorb the plant nutrients from the soil. Avoid applying fertilizer closer than 2 to 3 feet from the trunk.

7

MAJOR TREE GENERA

LIST OF TREE GENERA

Flowering Plants (Magnoliophyta; Angiosperms)

Dicotyledons (Magnoliopsida; broadleaf or hardwood trees)

- Anacardiaceae (Cashew family)
- Cashew, *Anacardium occidentale*
- Mango, *Mangifera indica*
- Pistachio, *Pistacia vera*
- Sumac, *Rhus* species
- Lacquer tree, *Toxicodendron verniciflua*
- Annonaceae (Custard apple family)
- Cherimoya *Annona cherimola*
- Custard apple *Annona reticulata*
- Pawpaw *Asimina triloba*
- Soursop *Annona muricata*
- Apocynaceae (Dogbane family)
- Pachypodium *Pachypodium* species

- Aquifoliaceae (Holly family)
- Holly, *Ilex* species
- Araliaceae (Ivy family)
- Kalopanax, *Kalopanax pictus*
- Betulaceae (Birch family)
- Alder, *Alnus* species
- Birch, *Betula* species
- Hornbeam, *Carpinus* species
- Hazel, *Corylus* species
- Bignoniaceae (family)
- Catalpa, *Catalpa* species
- Cactaceae (Cactus family)
- Saguaro, *Carnegiea gigantea*
- Cannabaceae (Cannabis family)
- Hackberry, *Celtis* species
- Cornaceae (Dogwood family)
- Dogwood, *Cornus* species
- Dipterocarpaceae family
- Garjan *Dipterocarpus* species
- Sal *Shorea* species
- Ericaceae (Heath family)
- Arbutus, *Arbutus* species
- Eucommiaceae (Eucommia family)
- Eucommia *Eucommia ulmoides*
- Fabaceae (Pea family)
- Acacia, *Acacia* species
- Honey locust, *Gleditsia triacanthos*
- Black locust, *Robinia pseudoacacia*

- Laburnum, *Laburnum* species
- Pau Brasil, Brazilwood, *Caesalpinia echinata*
- Fagaceae (Beech family)
- Chestnut, *Castanea* species
- Beech, *Fagus* species
- Southern beech, *Nothofagus* species
- Tanoak, *Lithocarpus densiflorus*
- Oak, *Quercus* species
- Fouquieriaceae (Boojum family)
- Boojum, *Fouquieria columnaris*
- Hamamelidaceae (Witch-hazel family)
- Sweetgum, *Liquidambar* species
- Persian Ironwood, *Parrotia persica*
- Juglandaceae (Walnut family)
- Walnut, *Juglans* species
- Hickory, *Carya* species
- Wingnut, *Pterocarya* species
- Lauraceae (Laurel family)
- Cinnamon *Cinnamomum zeylanicum*
- Bay laurel *Laurus nobilis*
- Avocado *Persea americana*
- Lecythidaceae (Paradise nut family)
- Brazil Nut *Bertholletia excelsa*
- Lythraceae Loosestrife family
- Crape-myrtle *Lagerstroemia* species
- Magnoliaceae (Magnolia family)
- Tulip tree, *Liriodendron* species
- Magnolia, *Magnolia* species

- Malvaceae (Mallow family; including Tiliaceae and Bombacaceae)
- Baobab, *Adansonia* species
- Silk-cotton tree, *Bombax* species
- Bottletrees, *Brachychiton* species
- Kapok, *Ceiba pentandra*
- Durian, *Durio zibethinus*
- Balsa, *Ochroma lagopus*
- Cacao (cocoa), *Theobroma cacao*
- Linden (Basswood, Lime), *Tilia* species
- Meliaceae (Mahogany family)
- Neem, *Azadirachta indica*
- Bead tree, *Melia azedarach*
- Mahogany, *Swietenia mahagoni*
- Moraceae (Mulberry family)
- Fig, *Ficus* species
- Mulberry, *Morus* species
- Myristicaceae (Nutmeg family)
- Nutmeg, *Mysristica fragrans*
- Myrtaceae (Myrtle family)
- Eucalyptus, *Eucalyptus* species
- Myrtle, *Myrtus* species
- Guava, *Psidium guajava*
- Nyssaceae (Tupelo family; sometimes included in Cornaceae)
- Tupelo, *Nyssa* species
- Dove tree, *Davidia involucrata*
- Oleaceae (Olive family)

- Olive, *Olea europaea*
- Ash, *Fraxinus* species
- Paulowniaceae (Paulownia family)
- Foxglove Tree, *Paulownia* species
- Platanaceae (Plane family)
- Plane, *Platanus* species
- Rhizophoraceae (Mangrove family)
- Red Mangrove, *Rhizophora mangle*
- Rosaceae (Rose family)
- Rowans, Whitebeams, Service Trees *Sorbus* species
- Hawthorn, *Crataegus* species
- Pear, *Pyrus* species
- Apple, *Malus* species
- Almond, *Prunus dulcis*
- Peach, *Prunus persica*
- Plum, *Prunus domestica*
- Cherry, *Prunus* species
- Rubiaceae (Bedstraw family)
- Coffee, *Coffea* species
- Rutaceae (Rue family)
- Citrus, *Citrus* species
- Cork-tree, *Phellodendron* species
- Euodia, *Tetradium* species
- Salicaceae (Willow family)
- Aspen, *Populus* species
- Poplar, *Populus* species
- Willow, *Salix* species

- Sapindaceae (including Aceraceae, Hippocastanaceae) (Soapberry family)
- Maple, *Acer* species
- Buckeye, Horse-chestnut, *Aesculus* species
- Mexican Buckeye, *Ungnadia speciosa*
- Lychee, *Litchi sinensis*
- Golden rain tree, *Koelreuteria paniculata*
- Sapotaceae (Sapodilla family)
- Gutta-percha, *Palaquium* species
- Tambalacoque, or "dodo tree", *Sideroxylon grandiflorum, previously Calvaria major*
- Simaroubaceae family
- Tree of heaven, *Ailanthus* species
- Theaceae (Camellia family)
- Gordonia, *Gordonia* species
- Stuartia, *Stuartia* species
- Thymelaeaceae (Thymelaea family)
- Ramin, *Gonystylus* species
- Ulmaceae (Elm family)
- Elm, *Ulmus* species
- Zelkova, *Zelkova* species
- Verbenaceae family
- Teak, *Tectona* species

Monocotyledons (Liliopsida)

- Agavaceae (Agave family)
- Cabbage tree, *Cordyline australis*
- Dragon tree, *Dracaena draco*
- Joshua tree, Yucca brevifolia

- Arecaceae (Palmae) (Palm family)
- Areca Nut, *Areca catechu*
- Coconut *Cocos nucifera*
- Date Palm, *Phoenix dactylifera*
- Chusan Palm, *Trachycarpus fortunei*
- Poaceae (grass family)
- Bamboos Poaceae subfamily Bambusoideae

Note that banana 'trees' are not actually trees; they are not woody nor is the stalk perennial.

Conifers (Pinophyta; softwood trees)

- Araucariaceae (Araucaria family)
- Araucaria, *Araucaria* species
- Kauri, *Agathis* species
- Cupressaceae (Cypress family)
- Cypress, *Cupressus* species
- Cypress, *Chamaecyparis* species
- Juniper, *Juniperus* species
- Alerce or Patagonian cypress, *Fitzroya cupressoides*
- Sugi, *Cryptomeria japonica*
- Coast Redwood, *Sequoia sempervirens*
- Giant Sequoia, *Sequoiadendron giganteum*
- Dawn Redwood, *Metasequoia glyptostroboides*
- Bald Cypress, *Taxodium distichum*
- Pinaceae (Pine family)
- White pine, *Pinus* species
- Pinyon pine, *Pinus* species
- Pine, *Pinus* species
- Spruce, *Picea* species

- Larch, *Larix* species
- Douglas-fir, *Pseudotsuga* species
- Fir, *Abies* species
- Cedar, *Cedrus* species
- Podocarpaceae (Yellowwood family)
- African Yellowwood, *Afrocarpus falcatus*
- Totara, *Podocarpus totara*
- Sciadopityaceae
- Kusamaki, *Sciadopitys* species
- Taxaceae (Yew family)
- Yew, *Taxus* species

Ginkgos (Ginkgophyta)

- Ginkgoaceae (Ginkgo family)
- Ginkgo, *Ginkgo biloba*

Cycads (Cycadophyta)

- Cycadaceae family
- Ngathu cycad, *Cycas angulata*
- Zamiaceae family
- Wunu cycad, *Lepidozamia hopei*

Ferns (Pterophyta)

- Cyatheaceae and Dicksoniaceae families
- Tree ferns, *Cyathea, Alsophila, Dicksonia* (not a monophyletic group)

THE LIFE CYCLE OF TREES

The life cycles of trees, especially conifers, are divided into the following stages in forestry for survey and documentation purposes:

- Seed

- Seedling: the above ground part of the embryo that sprout from the seed
- Sapling: After the seedling reaches 1m tall, and until it reaches 7cm in stem diameter
- Pole: young trees from 7-30cm diameter
- Mature tree: over 30cm diameter, reproductive years begin
- Old tree: dominate old growth forest; height growth slows greatly, with majority of productivity in seed production
- Overmature: dieback and decay become common
- Snag: standing dead wood
- Log/debris: fallen dead wood

Index

❑❑❑